· THE BEETLE LEG

the

beetle

leg

BY JOHN HAWKES

A NEW DIRECTIONS BOOK

Typography by Sophie Hawkes

MANUFACTURED IN THE UNITED STATES OF AMERICA

Published in Canada by Penguin Books Canada Limited

New Directions Books are published for James Laughlin

by New Directions Publishing Corporation

80 Eighth Avenue, New York 10011

Eighth Printing

FOR MY MOTHER AND FATHER

THE SHERIFF

quarius is poor. Sagit-
tarius is poor. Virgo is a Barren Sign, it will produce no growth. The
first day the Moon is in a Sign is better than the second and the sec-
ond better than the third. Seed planted when the Earth is in Leo,
which is a Barren, Fiery Sign, will die, as it is favorable only to the
destruction of noxious growth. Trim no trees or vines when the Moon
or Earth is in Leo. For they will surely die.

He stopped reading, marked his place, and began to talk.

It is a lawless country.

For fourteen years I've watched it with my boys, and not one year
has passed without a thieving or a disturbance caught up like some
bad notion by our townsmen. Man and woman, out here at least, don't
learn to keep to their own houses of a night. I've found them, plenty
of them, faces that I knew, some I didn't know, in the most unlikely
lots or ditches or clear under a porch. If I didn't find them first there
were others did. I slept light, waiting for those to come and tell me.

There was one death.

But a man gets used to a pair of handcuffs on his hip. The string our tank key is hung from—we only got the one cell—has been around my neck the entire fourteen years. And there's not one shirt I own but what it's got badge holes through the pocket. Some men don't commit crimes, but they're ready to. I've had two ranchers come to me in the middle of the night with a horse between them, and they trusted me to know whose horse it was. A man gets used to staying around a jail. I did. And there's one thing sure; it'll never have to hold no woman. There are other rooms in town for that.

I used to follow the tracks of a single horse for miles in my pickup truck and that man I trailed—there were only a few prints in the sand like someone stirred it with a stick—had committed a violation, was running all the time I drove. Or I was called to pay a visit to some woman who discovered a man on her place. I wore my cartridge belt summer or winter and my sleeves rolled up.

It was the men or women who didn't have no place to hide that gave me trouble. Them people too easy found doing things a man can't talk about, things that happened or not depending on whether you arrived five minutes early or five late. They broke the law all right, directly they couldn't quiet down and talk when I was near enough to see. It almost depended on how much white showed from the side of the road before my torch was even lit. I took them in. I've got no time to waste with men like that.

But I never caught them Lampson brothers at it. Others I have. There's families in this country, where there's a daughter or son and daughter—or perhaps even a young mother without children, or a widow—and they're the ones that have forced my hand. I ain't keen on nodding at the father or husband when it's over, either. I don't like to see a man who's got to count heads all night—or who takes to going out himself.

But not the Lampson boys. No one ever even thought they had

done one thing to shame us, at least not before the older married. And the younger's record is still clear.

I used to know the younger well.

It's not easy holding reins on people, keeping watch. There's something about a single street, some houses and four or five hundred square miles of ground that seems to make them worse. A hand comes in off a ranch, yellowed, with his mouth still closed, and there's no way of telling what he's done. It takes hours to find out. I didn't even meet the younger Lampson until the day his brother married. I went to that wedding.

But two years before, I saw the older.

In my job a man's teeth start to grind, his jaws don't seem to set well when he's got to write up warrants and serve them too. It's a day's work to stop cars, take strangers by the elbow, and see public places closed on time. And I had to identify them. A man's eyes burn, he ain't too comfortable when he has got to stand in front of his own cell door, to stare at the one who is now inside and won't even look you in the face. Or worse, wants to talk. Why, when a person has a visitor in town, harmless enough for some, perhaps, I've got to ask around if I hear about it. You never really know if they're relatives or even friends. A different window burning in a house at night —anything could happen. You take to drinking coffee and know how full or empty the local courtroom is going to be before you even get there. And it's often. A man gets kind of sick at the law when he don't know who has come into town or left it.

But the day I saw him I was feeling good. Nothing could have bothered me when I first saw the older Lampson. I was just Deputy at the time. Just barely hanging onto and still learning about the harm that is done right in a kitchen or in an open field.

I took the call. And that cheered the day for me because it was only the voice of a little girl, and I suppose I thought to hear of a killing or of a man with his hand pierced on a fork. "Honey," I told her, "I'll come over." If she had been grown, I would have considered more. It wasn't far to drive. I think though of how far that little girl must have walked, in a bathing suit, and I don't know as I could stand it now. Whoever owned that telephone didn't even help her or else she just wanted to make the call herself.

It was twenty mile but I had my truck.

I remember a day like that. There was nothing really wrong; I found her at the roadside, standing bareheaded and with thin hair, in a sun as heavy as I ever saw. She wore one of them square bathing suits, pinched high like she had it awhile, with straight wide straps pulled across her shoulders. As soon as I parked the car and locked it, and without moving, she spoke:

"I got a friend. She's holding him."

That's all. She turned and led the way toward the nearby river.

In those days, before they choked her off, that river widened or narrowed as it pleased, one day going fast, the next slow. But no matter how it flowed and until it dried, it carried its own high load of mud and a body lost upstream or down would have been hid for good. I knew children shouldn't play around it.

But they run loose out here like their parents. And you can't tell what children see or what they find. They're skinned up and bandaged from climbing around where people big enough to do wrong have done it, or tried to, since sometimes me and my boys can stop them before they're through. Right in the middle of the desert where there is hardly sign of bird or animal you are liable to find some scrap or garment that once belonged personally to a woman. That's evidence. A man is wise if he keeps to town. But even there he comes across it.

So I walked quiet as I could when I first smelled that brown water and caught sight of the shadows from shrub and cactus that grew more heavy in those days, when the crime rate was high around the river and the daylight offenders were the worst. I knew this little girl had found one of the spots where water, meant just to liven up men half dead or draw together cattle, drives men and women to undress and swim and maybe kill themselves. That water towed under many.

I've dragged it. That was part of my job, as well as bringing out liquor to a horse with heaves or holding a basin under a man's wrists that was slashed in jail. He lived. I hate the sight of a dragging iron with all them rusty points that you lower from the end of a slippery rope. We never caught much with it anyway. I don't like boats.

This time we didn't need an iron. And I didn't figure to have to use my gun, not with this child safe enough to come and get me, leaving her friend to wait. But I had it ready.

The shrubbery didn't cover us at all. I think he saw us from the first. I didn't care if he did; the thing to do was to crouch down as we was and watch before jumping up to scare him or chase him away. I took my time. There are other times when you have to step right in, when you are Sheriff or even Deputy, and catch hold of a bare shoulder or head of hair, keeping your face turned back so as it don't get bruised, and drag them off. Maybe you get splashed with a glass of beer or your hand gets bit, but they have to be broke apart. Fast. I would rather help a woman have a baby than fight with them that don't or that don't care. But sometimes it's better not to move.

We watched.

We sat there in the sun like we had fish poles and all day to wait for what would happen, like that little girl and me would have supper when we got back and it could keep, with no trouble at home, until we did.

But the one we watched—he must have had his fish already. He looked fit. Fit enough to swim the river at least instead of squatting on the other bank. I think that girl knew it too. He might not have bolted either had I got right up and hollared at him. He liked it where he was. The girl pointed to her friend who sat alone on the sand about half way out a spit that stuck into the river but didn't join the other side. It was the spot he would make for. If he decided to try.

"She's afraid."

"And you ain't?" I whispered back. The towhead girl—plenty of our children out here have white hair, usually not cut too even—was drawing in the sand. Now and then she kind of pulled at her bathing suit or twisted her head and back like she might if she was older or like she wanted to get up and run.

As far as I could see, he didn't care. He seemed to be staring at the water. I might have had him in the jail house, there was nothing about him said I couldn't. On the other hand, there was nothing stamped him bad. I know when to bide my temper and just size up the stride of a man or the way he hangs back when you ask him what he is at. I tried to make out what his hands were doing, but he had them hid. I didn't suspect him much, though I'd like to have seen if they were small and kind of pink with short tapering fingers.

He wasn't suspecting either. He didn't know how close I watch a man. I lit my pipe, seeing he wouldn't go no matter what. I've seen all kinds, men I had to drive out and below town myself, set them down and make sure they headed south out of sight; others I caught before they entered. And if I stop a couple, I may let them go, I may not. You got to watch them if they are in pair.

But I have never seen one just squatting in the desert. He's not sick, more like he's healthier than most around here. Most men stop

12

at a river bank to drink, cool their feet, and get across and be done with it. Here's a man, I thought, is snarled with this river. He'll have more trouble with it yet, I figured.

There wasn't any tree to give him shade. You might see a man like him on an island—him and that opposite bank started to look that way to me—someone who had been left there or thrown ashore and you wouldn't know whether to go up to him or not. It was too late to hail him now. I couldn't bring myself to do it.

But I wasn't going to leave him there to do what he pleased. And he was set for something, because his pants were off, already rolled up and slung over his shoulder when we got there. My pipe went out and I found I was watching him so hard I sat chewing on it dry. He still wore his suspenders—bright yellow like a shirt I owned but which no Deputy could ever wear—and they just hung down, unfastened.

If there had been any kind of house around, I might have understood. But there he was, casting a small patch of shadow on water so dark it hardly showed, a man who didn't look ready to cause trouble and didn't seem to be got up for any kind of work. He was only half dressed and certainly alone, and yet he didn't look to need no bothering. The towhead wasn't minding him, I could see that.

I'm quick to feel out a stranger. In my job you find that other men ain't like yourself, not when they open their mouths and you see they got no teeth or pull out a billfold filled with too much money or none at all. Most men is soft and childish or else they got to tell you something behind the house. For all I knew he was only looking at his picture in the water. It finally came to me I wasn't going to sit there and wait for him.

"Honey," I said, "I can't arrest that man." She didn't answer. If I did, the jail would be full of them, men who have come home on foot or men just walking aways from a ranch they never left and that

I ain't happened to have seen before. We had too many in them days anyway. "He ain't hurt," I said. "He ain't drunk. I don't think he's got a gun. That's enough." But he was something to stare at for an hour or two.

Either he's a man escaped already from another prison, where he stayed in the fields or worked out on the roads—and that wasn't likely—or else he comes naturally by his skin to stand the burn marks of such a sun. And that's good. He had no hat. I can sit or even stand in it myself the whole day without my mind becoming clouded or even getting up a thirst. I could see that he could too. But there is a limit, when it seemed he didn't want to talk.

I whispered, "Ain't it time to go?"

"No," she answered.

"Well, we are," I said. Maybe he was looking at them little girls, the one hardly hid behind a thorn, the other sitting on her thin legs out there in the sand, maybe not. He must have felt as queer coming across two children that way as they did seeing a grown man perched down like he was on the edge of a river quiet. I don't know what he thought when he saw me.

I figured that maybe if I stood up he would. He didn't. I made the girl get up and brush the sand off herself too. When I stretch out, as I did then, I'm tall enough for a man to see me. I looked right at him, at his shirt tails that was as good as pants to another, at the easy way he slouched as if, had there been some driftwood within reach, he might have built a fire. He was young.

"I'll drive you girls home," I told them, "you'll be missed."

I thought that when we turned and walked away he would stop playing at us and swim across. I would have taken him in my car that day. Men sometimes misjudge a route out here, they're liable to stray miles. They're lucky if they get a ride.

He stayed.

He probably had a car himself, I never learned. He might have had it parked back behind a dune where I thought the country was flat as it is most everywhere; he probably found a hollow and hid it there with all the things he carried and everything that made him what he was inside it.

That's where I should have looked for trouble.

●

a man lay buried just below the water level of the dam. He was embedded in the earth and entangled with a caterpillar, pump engine and a hundred feet of hose, somewhere inside the mountain that was protected from the lake on one side by rock and gravel and kept from erosion on its southward slope by partially grown rows of yellow grass. This man—he was remembered in Mistletoe, Government City, and would be as long as the Great Slide came to mind with every ale case struck open—was the brother of one who still hung on, having a place in the fields southwest of the official lines of the town. Boundaries were still marked with transit stakes ten years old.

In the sunset the survivor of the two, who had not taken part in the battle of the river and who had been on the range when the Slide occurred, drove his team of four horses across the sand of the southward slope, the machine under his seat spitting out seeds, grinding its unaligned rods. His voice carried all the way to the town on the bluff. He rode the boards holding the dry lines in one hand and a flattened cigarette pinched in the other, one knee cocked up and his hat pulled low over blackened cheeks and chin. Six days a week he nursed the animals across the sunward, dry side of the dam for twenty-five dollars a day, and the wind blew sand in his ears and blew the horses' manes the wrong way. A few hundred yards above his head, from the sharp-rocked track across the top of the dam, the dark, rarely fished miles of water narrowed into a cone through the hills of the badlands. Below him, in the middle of the mosquito flat and at the edge of the man-made delta and surrounded by piles of iron pipe and small, corrugated iron huts, red lead painted sections of the half completed turbine tower rose among steel girders spiked with insulators and weighted with hundreds of high tension, lead-in wires.

The day shift of the Metal and Lumber Company had stopped work an hour ago, and now the cowboy drove his team without the firing of the riveters or torches blasting sand from the air. For a moment the sun touched the black mounds of earth behind the tower and drifted off, down the almost dry channel as far as he could see, where once the wide river would have lost its mud color and changed to orange, then purple, in the days before Mistletoe even existed and when the fishing was good any place he sat down to cast.

When he heard a shrill faraway whistle in Clare, twenty miles away, he climbed down, unhitched the team, left the old machine for the night still dropping a few seeds, and let the horses tug him easily toward home on the end of the reins. For a whole day he had been sowing flowers, back and forth, on the mile long stretch of his brother's grave, and now the horses were tired and he was thirsty. Man and animals cut down from the crest of the dam to the high weeded plateau, basined in the rear by the long gravel approach and fronting on the filled in section of the horseshoe town. Soon the crest would be topped with a macadam road and the street lamps, if ever wired and the last switches installed, would be lit against the horizon.

The four brown dray horses chomped slowly across the dry track, swaying in the rear but shaking their round noses and twitching their ears in excitement, stumbling now and then in a hole by the road so heavily that it seemed they must fall. Passing one prong of the few hundred brown houses of Mistletoe, Luke Lampson waved to the Finn, a crippled ex-bronc rider hammering on a stoop with two white canes.

Then, digging his long heels into the turf, he pulled the horses as a station wagon swung close, raising the dust. He waved again, this time at the tin helmeted Metal and Lumber night shift men, setting off to throw sparks from the tower until dawn. He followed the thin sticks hung from a string of barbed wire through the darkening fields, slapping at the mosquitoes that bit through his pants, until, after once more placing a few light logs across the gate, he could look down on the plank and tar paper buildings of his ranch. He turned the horses loose and they trotted downhill, for all their age like young dogs.

"Slow down there," he called, afraid that they would hit the wire in the darkness and skin open their broad two-sided chests. He splashed water on his face at the washstand by the house and looked over the bare country toward Mistletoe. He could see the light of fine sparks from the tower; they were at work already.

Only a few mile twists of wire sheared the damp land into fields and made it claim to a farm, a ranch, a fallen barn. Phosphorescent clumps of weed and sage rolled airily in sight, but lone animals moved invisibly though a hoof click on stone carried for miles through the warm evening.

Mosquitoes beat against the inside and outside of the windows and Luke Lampson's horses thudded out of range of the house and, motionless, hung their heads over the furthest stretch of wire. Luke stomped up the steps, two potato sacks filled with sand, pushed open the door wobbling on leather hinges, and walked across the leaning floor to the bunk on his bowed, tightly denimed, tired legs.

"Evening, Ma," he said and pulled off the cracked, square-toed, lady-size cowboy boots. And, more tiredly, under his breath:

"Evening, Maverick," and he glanced once at the Mandan who squatted by the dusty blanket hanging from the foot of the bunk. The black hair hung over her face.

The woman at the wood stove shook the skillet and it spit on the red iron.

"What's the matter, Ma, you out of sorts?"

"Not so's anybody'd see."

Luke lay back on the pile of covers and, lighting a short end of cigarette, flipped the wooden match to a tin can of water on the far side of the room. A pair of antlers, patches of hair and dried skin stuck to the yellow bone chip of skull, hung crookedly on the wall above the can. An old branch lay cradled in the horns. Luke rubbed his feet together—even in summer he wore thick-woven socks—and, with the toes of one foot sticking through a long raveling hole, scratched. The Mandan, crouching out of sight and never smiling, reached up one dark arm and with a long stem of hay tickled at the bare toes. But the black little feet, tough with rocks and hot with sand, did not feel it. He went on smoking.

"At least you could make her help. Me doing all this heavy work."

"Go on, Maverick, give her a hand."

The Indian climbed slowly to her feet, pulled down her red sweater, smoothed her faded, straw covered plaid skirt and padding to the open shelves, reached for thick lipped cups and plates. Her charm bracelets jangled as each piece of china was set heavily on the dark planks of the table. She kept out of the stove woman's way.

"That's the one job I like doing myself." Ma splattered onions in the pan. "Light work. And I never get to do it."

"Go fetch some water," Luke said to the girl. "Shut the door," he called. It remained open and mosquitoes hummed in and out.

"I ain't here the whole day long," Luke swung his feet to the floor. "I don't see what's to keep you from sprawling right here on this bunk from sunup to dark. If you want." Luke's face, black with the sun, would fit a palm of the woman's hand and when he rocked across the floor it caught the fire from the stove. He rolled like a child playing sailor, loosening his neckerchief.

Ma shook her head. "That's where she sneaks off to. I couldn't do it." The Mandan returned with the load of water; she carried the bucket almost as lightly as the older woman, who could lug six brimming gallons the whole mile long trail as easily as two pint jars of honey. Reaching under the bunk, the Indian pulled out her dusty, high heeled, patent leather store shoes. She squeezed them onto bare feet and sat down to table. She ate from the edge of the knife, her black sides of hair falling into the bowl of food. Now and then she watched the cowboy scowling into his mug behind the hurricane lamp.

Ma never sat to any meal. She kept her back to the world and her face toward the red range, toward the cartons of matches, the row of pans and long handled forks. Sometimes she pushed the lid off the skillet and stole a bite on a long blackened prong or a sip from a wooden spoon. She refilled their plates without turning around. But the Mandan had to pour the coffee.

The deep dish skillet, as big around as a butter tub, was never off the stove and the flames were never allowed to die from under it. The fat was rarely changed and it boiled and snapped from one month to the next. Whether it was a piece of fish dropped into it or a slab of beef pulled out, it tasted of the black countryside. Tempered by the heat of wood coals, warming the room itself in winter, the skillet was slated over with layer on layer of charred mineral, encrusted with drippings, accumulating from the inside out fragments of every meal. Not a night went by but what Ma, quickly awakened in the darkness, got up to feed the fire and make sure the skillet burned. It was Ma's pot, the iron of her life, to which came the pickings of her garden, the produce of her monthly shopping trips to Clare, the eggs she got each morning from the coop and whatever Luke might bring home at night—rhubarb, apples or a quarter head of cabbage. She kept it steaming.

Ma was not Luke Lampson's mother. Hattie Lampson now lay buried on the bluff where once the tents were pitched. Ma had married, to the south in Clare and when the project was first conceived, Luke's older brother, the Lampson incarcerated in the dam. Sometimes, rarely, wearing rubber boots and a shawl and carrying an egg basket, she would walk the high shoulder of mud, rock and gravel, and look down the water toward the badlands.

"You never knew nothing about it," she told Luke, "you were out where it was dry. You never even saw the Great Slide." She moved the skillet a little off the fire.

Luke got up from the table and looked at the Mandan. "You do those dishes for Ma. You hear?" She leaned on the boards, hid her face behind her hands and went on eating.

"She never says anything when I'm around." Ma licked at the edge of the spoon and opened the draft a notch.

"You just don't understand how she speaks, that's all." Luke undid his belt and shuffled among a pile of men and women's clothing until he found a fresh black and white checked shirt. He pulled on his best pair of boots and polished the toes with the blanket tip.

22

Smelling of hair oil—the Mandan groomed herself from the same bottle—he rolled the brim of his hat, wiped at the sweatband, and drew it sharply over his eyes. He hopped to the ground over the potato sacks with the same jump and spring with which he used to run across the barn dance floor when the river was still indefinitely harnessed and the proposed streets on the bluff were not approved by the central office. He stood in the light of the hurricane lamp and ahead, above the rise in the darkness where his own place ended, he saw the small glow in the sky, as if far into the plains a few branders crouched by embers and sets of cooling irons.

"Them boys are flaring up tonight for sure," he said and, whistling through his teeth, stepped out of sight. The night shift men were on the scaffold welding and below, by an iron hut, Harry Bohn put a pot of coffee back on the fire and prepared to return to Mistletoe.

Ma turned from her skillet and called out. "Don't you say anything against Mulge. I won't have it!"

He was almost to the gate logs in the wire and he looked back once at the ranch house, through the door that appeared to open on an empty room. Against the mosquito horizon he made out the high, thick logged, stockade-like breaking corral and a moldy Mexican saddle athwart the top-most beam. He could have seen the slanting, tack room shack and the chicken rest behind, but between the horse and fowl structures and the ranch house itself there lay a patch of darkness broad enough to hide two dung wagons end to end or a pack of dogs.

They were waiting for him there. Each strap in place, not a buckle rattled. The Red Devils sat their machines quietly and their gloved hands waited over switches, ready to twist the handle grips for speed. They sat straight, tilted slightly forward, faces hidden by drawn goggles and fastened helmets, the front wheels in an even row all leaning to the left as tight polished boots raised, rested lightly on the starting pedals. The straight, grounded left legs were parallel in black flaring britches and from the several creatures sitting double, with arms locked patiently around wood hard belts, there was never a murmur. Not a foot slipped nor did the saddle springs creak. Between the empty corral and the woman's kitchen the motorcycles filled the darkness, the first almost touching the logs and the last within arm's length of the cardboard wall. The black, deep-grooved tires were clean and hard. It was as if they had made no flying circuits that evening nor left rubber burns and cuts in the sand where few humans gather, in the gullies of rattlesnakes or before the coils of braided whips. Their saddlebags were still unopened, they had not slept. They watched as hunters by a pond in the marsh from which a single old bird, flapping and beating across the flat water, is unable to rise. License plates had been stripped from the mudguards.

Luke Lampson walked on a dry ridge in the middle of the wagon track. After a quarter mile through failing truck gardens and stony sand, he met the asphalt highway, heard pebbles shake loose under the thistle, a scratching in the brambles. A thin lizard leaped from the ridge and away down the brown clay rut.

A breeze came from the funnel of badlands. Cooled across the water, it was warmed as soon as it touched these acres rising and falling from the boundary of the dam in flats and hollows. At times he could smell the fresh, exposed side of the mountain that had been under the water line all day. A buried man now drained above the tide. Luke wondered if his body ever shifted in the sand, he thought of it when seeding. "Someday he'll worm himself right out to the open air," the cowboy said. "Mighty like he's crawling around in there right now, winding his way up toward the side I've sown." The

24

whistle bleated beyond Gov City and the Metal and Lumber men climbed down.

Luke Lampson stopped to light up a Personally-Rolled. It was a long walk across three provinces.

Where the scuff country met the broad back of the highway and little clumps of sand and weed were kept from spreading by the long raised shoulder of the road, there, nosed to the edge of the empty speed lanes, he saw the head and taillights of a parked car. It was long. Between the yellow glare of fog and headlights and the blinking red danger arrows in the rear, stretched the darkness that was the car itself, too long to house in any ordinary driveway. Luke knew that on its sloping top, in aluminum racks, would be the airplane luggage, built up like blocks and, neatly strapped and rolled on top of it all, the tree green unused camping tent. Fresh wooden tent stakes, tied with clean white fishing line, would never be taken from the rear compartment.

"Tourists," he thought. "One of those big black tires has let them down. They don't know whether to spit on it or buy another." The front light beams carried for two hundred yards and in that full white incandescence he could see the fence posts and a crooked, hand painted *Poison Water* sign.

A man and woman crouched before the solid radiator in the light. They were holding something between them.

"Wrong," thought Luke, "guess they've hit a dog. Or maybe a jack rabbit. Probably never seen them that big before." He stepped over the wire, pushing it down between the rusted barbs, and shielded his eyes.

"He's been bit," said Camper, the owner of the car, and glanced at the boy between his knees. The man Camper wore a yellow, large collared shirt with even tails worn outside the flannel trousers. He watched Luke through dark cat-eye glasses and puffed in fast heavy breaths.

His wife loosed her perfume on the air as if she carried a broken phial of it in a hidden pocket of the green silk slacks. She got out of their way.

"You see, I had to stop. There weren't any roadstands or hotels, not a light anywhere. So I just pulled off the road and stepped out of the light and then the kid has to come out too. For two hundred miles I wouldn't stop, not with warning signs posted every fifty feet. It's a hell of a thing when you can't take a leak without kicking up a pack of rattlers." His white socks bulged through the braided sandals and he slapped his arms.

The boy looked as if he had been dropped in a bucket of cold water.

Luke pushed his hat on the back of his head, and taking the tin box from his rear pocket, squatted opposite but close to Camper. The woman waited in the car, raising and lowering the aerial, pushing one station button after the next and heard only a squall of electricity on iron ore.

"I can see you ain't from around here," said Luke. He squinted into the light, fixed the blade into the little handle and draped the short length of hose, used as a siphon by some of the men in Clare, across his knee.

"Like hell," answered the driver. "I know where I am. I used to work around here, but the wife doesn't know it. Let me tell you, I practically built that dam alone. Yes, sir, I remember still, the 'cheapest earth filled dam in the western hemisphere' it was supposed to be. And the Slide—I suppose you know about it—was like a whole corner of the world fell in."

"I recollect it," said Luke.

"I was surprised not to find any lights, not even a lunch wagon on the road." The driver leaned closer to watch. "I must've missed the turning into town. 'There isn't any town way out here,' says my wife, but I know better. I thought we'd just fly through for a quick look around. And of course to stop some place. I was surprised to see the place so run down, not a sign or anything. Why, you wouldn't even know the dam was here."

"It's here all right," said Luke.

He twisted up the leg, tied the rubber hose so that the lower calf went white and the upper darkened, making the child appear ready for transfusion. Keeping the blade out of the child's sight, he peered at the fang marks in the coloring flesh. A crack of static burst from the car. "Try another station, Lou," called Camper and they heard the whirr as the window was rolled shut.

His tin kit lay open in the dust at his heels, the extra blade catching the light, the label worn off the green corked bottle of iodine. Luke squeezed the leg, satisfied himself with the set of punctures, tightened the rubber tubing, shifted a bit, took up a packet of matches and, striking three or four, heated the blade.

Luke had seen them stricken before: Ma was not immune to rattlers on the water trail and even the Mandan was struck one blow from a startled head. The snakes were driven further and further from the bluff and new highway, and gathered wherever a few rocks or sticks could hide them deeper in the fields. He had killed them with rake handles. Once he ground an old flathead down with his long heel. But still their bodies might dart from a forkful of hay or dash from under pail or wheel to strike.

The blade turned blue. Luke once more picked up the leg and sank the point quickly in and out until two crosses had been cut and, the knife still hanging from his fingers, Camper holding the child's shoulders, he relaxed his face and posture and sucked the wounds, his eyes growing heavy in the headlights, staring, as if the venom had a hard and needy taste to a man who, in all his youth on the infested range, had never himself been bitten. He took it as one of his four drays copped the bar of salt, hung over it, and kept it from the rest.

Specks of red appeared on Camper's yellow shirt and with one hand he swatted, all the while watching the cowboy draw, turn, spit and stoop again. The mosquitoes filtered across the headlight, hummed and settled, biting into the driver's white arms and neck. "Hurry up," called the woman, her voice muffled behind the glass.

"This country's hell on a man," said Camper. He lit a cigarette and sat down more comfortably on the curving bumper. He watched the cowboy repack the tin and wipe his hands. "By the way," he rubbed his arms, "how deep is she these days?"

"Eighteen feet, six inches round noon," answered Luke, "but she's down a little now."

"That's a lot of water." He reached for his pocket. "I hate to be shoving off. Kind of like to wait until dawn and take a look around. I know there's fishing. But the wife'll be howling how she wants a hotel with screens on the windows and a girl to bring in the towels and washing water. Wait a minute," he looked at Luke's boots with steer heads carved above the ankles. "Can I give you something?"

"Naw. You just come back sometime when the sun's up and it's been raining a few days before. Come back and see her when she's brimming!"

"I will," called Camper, "I sure will."

Luke Lampson finally walked into the dark acres adjoining the few lamps and measured streets of Mistletoe. Approached from almost any side, it was open country, sand, clay and nests of weed; the horseshoe street was swept abruptly from a rutted field. Children's dolls and slides always lay toward the flagpole center, never behind the houses on the plain. Luke entered town by picking his way between two single story cabins and crossing the street before him to the drugstore: Estrellita's. He straightened his hat, brushed the burrs from his pants and pushed through the patched screen door.

"Howdy, Lampson, howdy, Lampson," murmured and softly echoed the men around oilclothed tables.

"Evening, gentlemen."

He crossed to the counter and settled himself on a chromium stool.

"A bottle of pop, Mary Jane," he said to the little girl in apron and white soda fountain cap.

Luke hooked his heels on a rung, spread his sharp knees and leaned over the straw. His back was to the men, his head hidden under the curled black brim. He looked into the rear kitchenette where an old man fried hamburgers and the girl did her lessons; he looked through the connecting door to the billiard room and back to his drink. There was only one light in the billiard hall, a pair of feet on the edge of a table and the row of cues. On the few nights of the week when a customer might enter, beer was served him and the light turned up. But those men who used to pride themselves on studied shots and drop ashes on the green cloth, now took to Estrellita's. They watched the cowboy, his stooped shoulders, the split in his shirt, the white calf of his leg between the top of the boot and the rolled denim.

"Any of you boys seen Bohn?"

They waited a moment and then: "Naw, Luke, not tonight."

"Ain't seen him since an hour."

"Reckon he's in to Clare."

The little girl laughed, pulled the primer over her face and the chef slammed a handful of meat on the griddle. With the point of his knife he pierced the bun, slit it, laid it flat and smeared on margarine. They heard the meatcake sizzling.

Across from Estrellita's was the Metal and Lumber Gymnasium where the welders played the linesmen, where raffles were held and any entertainment, resulting in proceeds for the town, occurred. The grilled windows were open, lights were strung over the slippery hardwood, the instrumentalists followed the scores of their sheet music bought in Clare. Luke paid his dime at the door.

he's here," said Wade of the man with the red wagon.

"Saw him, did you?"

"Yes, sir, I got a look at him."

There was a desk and a chair on rollers for the Sheriff of Clare and a cane chair for his visitor. But both men stood. In the jail office they did not face each other, rather they waited side by side, the Sheriff's hand on the other's arm, talking slowly, not quite in whispers. They did not move but rested on their feet, alert by standing, old now, steady, for nights which kept them from slumbering, together watchful, dimly awake.

"I knew he was coming, Wade. I heard of it." The Sheriff gently laid down the fat, wingfolded body of his Stetson.

No move was made to sit or turn and take the few steps to the open door from which they could have seen a street, a ridge of roof, the sloping, dry and distant night. Their backs remained without effort toward those sights, dim or broad, which might have made them think men slept in safety. Facing walls, the rear of the jail, they breathed together with a faint heave as if pollen and dust tracked them—all day they inhaled the clouds raised by a passing few youths —and the air were still laden long after the setting of the sun. They waited, come to a stop in the middle of the narrow stone room where dried cigarettes lay strewn on the faded blotter of the half open desk, where a winter coat hung from a peg, and the arm of each was made easy by touching the other's. A thin light hung above their heads from a long cord more rope than wire. Separately they stared at the floor, pausing a moment in those outer, less confining parts of a jail. They smiled.

"I guess someone will send for you, if there's need at all."

"No. I think you better get him, Wade."

Slowly, without looking back, they walked toward the center of the building, down a corridor to the complete darkness of the cell. They reached the coolness of that last room, divided in half and from the glow of the night by bars, and could be no longer hailed from the street. One side cell, the other bare, with iron rods embedded in the floor and ceiling, it was a room in which two men might meet out of town and in which, once before, a hanging had occurred from scarce planks, a hasty rope, and behind a canvas sheet still wet with turpentine and daubs of paint.

Smoke hardly rose from burning corn silk, no smell of tar or soap. Yet by the tank door—locked—the large shadows of the Sheriff and his friend, allowed owners of the cage, were free to lean against the metal, hold to greasy iron and hear the tinkering of jacknife, the strapping of wrists and tying of the hood. Wind, sand, bugs and daily voices rose and fell sealed beyond the walls of tin and white-washed brick. The two of them were spread, like men leaning over a fence, against the open slender rails of the tank.

"Wade, let's take a look at her." The voice, the rubbing, creasing sounds of the Sheriff drifted away from bars cool to the forehead. He stepped backwards, groped toward the wall and light cord. "She don't change." A match flared on his trousers, sulphur fumed in the darkness and for a moment Wade saw the bodies of sleeping prisoners on the tank room floor.

"Twelve years ago, Wade, I left this cell unguarded. And that night, when a break or most anything could have blown, I saw Luke Lampson. I spoke to him; I went along to see his brother married. And the jail held. She's just as strong tonight." He pulled the cord and both of them, waiting, rubbed their eyes. The Sheriff looked up, saw the gleam, specks of brown and black in the iron, the square slab of the lock. Wade interrupted.

"Sheriff, is them convicts?"

"Sure. But you know, Wade," again the hand lay on the other's arm, "I can't be in this room and touch these shining bars but what that wedding comes to mind and I see him."

"Sheriff. Tell me about these men. They're not just borrowing a place to sleep?"

"I caught them little devils tonight, Wade. Others are still loose. I think I'll let them go in the morning. They ain't much use to hold." He turned slowly, raised his eyes and settled his shoulder tightly between the bars, thrust his body into the pen. A swift prisoner could have caught and twisted the fat arm, an animal torn it with one slash. "I think of Luke right here. This is where I come back to, where I could remember straight, after the wedding. He wanted to come too; I didn't bring him. I wouldn't let him further than the office. There's not many like you, Wade, who want to hang around a jail, who have that need for the taste of lime and light that's different through ordinary window glass. I didn't know if to trust him. But ever after, Wade, this room's been full of fire. I like stone, a man of the law has got to like things hard; he's got to like the extra weight of a gun and the sound of a closing door. He's got to watch the men he guards when they're shaving from a basin on their knees. I was alone for weeks at that time. I didn't even leave the jail to eat.

"Wade, I wasn't the man to witness marriage. But he wanted it. We stood together, we pushed through all them women. And if I wanted I could have broke it up, I could have run the lot of them out of town. This cell here hasn't changed, it's just kept some of that celebration ever since the time I met him."

"Sheriff," Wade peered at the sleepers—one lay almost near enough to touch by stretching a restless foot—and his body slackened, fists settled heavily, arms rested high, "have they been fed?"

"Watered," continued the Sheriff in a voice low and wandering from the heat, "I watered them." The other nodded. "You know, Wade, I didn't even see his brother that night. Two years before I saw him though. I knew that he was marrying, but for all I care he didn't speak that night.

"But Luke spoke. By the time they had been married half an hour, with all those women trailing after them, and set maybe in some dark room with a latch on the door—I never cared to know where they spent that night—we were in the office, tipping easy together in our chairs. He could have been one of my boys right then, Wade. He was young enough. I could tell he liked it. But I sent him back and waited for morning by myself."

"You're not alone tonight, Sheriff. But, you sure these men ain't sick?"

"Wade, stop putting me off my thought. They're just locked up for the night is all." The Sheriff turned, placed his wide face between the bars so that they pressed on his temples and stared into the cell.

The prisoners did not rise. Occasional words, lights burning past the hour, caused no awakening fumble or sudden oath. A few Red Devils lay awkwardly spread eagle in the cell, the black driving mitten of one flung upon the seamless snout of another, tangled, sleeping, perhaps ready to spring with wild rubber limbs high and low against the bars. In captivity, sometime during the night, they had heaped themselves in the middle of the painted floor like a stack of slashed and darkened tires. The Sheriff and Wade slumped, grinned.

"Sheriff, watch this." Wade, beginning silently to shake, stooped and squeezed, pushed his leg recklessly through the bars. He puffed and it thrust forward, trousers sticking and riding up the bulky calf.

"Wade," the Sheriff chuckled and whispered, "you'll get it bit off."

The dusty shoe of a full sized man probed toward the small formless foot of the nearest sprawled prisoner. Wade hung low and twisted, stopped breathing and bent his head to aim. The Sheriff waited.

He kicked, then kicked again and suddenly pulling and swaying with all his weight he cursed, strained and drew it back. The Devil's foot moved a few inches and lay still.

"Hell," Wade caught his breath, "they're harmless."

"I told you. But, Wade," the fingers pressed, relaxed, "go get him for me."

The red wagon stood at the end of the street. Now and then a volley of firecrackers burst from a huddle of black braided Indians and with a dismal but high pitched cry they scattered, then returned panting toward the wagon. Or a single brave, eyes closed and ankle shoes clumping in the dust, would break from the rest and race with terrified showy speed away from the leaning red spectacle of the traveling house, straight up the center of the empty street.

The fireworks were old. Hoarded in leantos and one room cabins among families of fifteen children and ancient long haired eagle men, they were unearthed, armfuls brought into the street, supplied by bareback riders with pockets stuffed, lathered in haste. The paper cartridges exploded with stored energy or fizzled dangerously in clouds of smoke, the breath of a long horned animal on its knees. Above the clamor of the young men—their legs worked to the rattling of dry stones—the oldest Indian alive, without eyes, chin wrinkled into the mouth, clothed in baggy coat on the shoulders of which scraped his yellowed hair, stood rigidly still and, smiling or grimacing, waved in jerky circles a hissing sparkler.

One of the runners who had left with shouts and returned in a low scuffle, emerged from the alleys between the main buildings of Clare and quietly, whispering, crept to the front of the wagon to hold a bag of gray kernels under the strange horse's nose. Suddenly it thrashed its tail and ate.

The women of the tribe were waiting. Just beyond range of a sooted and yellow lantern that had been lighted, fanned, and set crookedly near the pair of weathered steps dropped on hinges from the back of the wagon, they bundled together and their brown skeletal cheekbones now and then twitched with pain. Their blank eyes turned upwards to the low but thick red door.

The wagon consisted of four rear wheels, extra high, and a little two windowed hut daubed with one barn color coat of paint. A tin chimney, that could be removed and wired to the side, stuck abruptly from the center of the sharp pointed roof and poured a fresh, foreign smelling smoke into the hot night air. It mixed with whiffs of gunpowder. Large, outsized shutters, stolen from a Victorian estate and thick enough to be bulletproof, were nailed across the windows. The house wagon was rough, gaudy, a small fortress of unmatched parts, with an air about it of harsh and lonely ill-repute. It was a cramped and wandering hovel. Yet high over the horse's sloping rump, the driver's seat was draped with a soft silk-haired sheepskin. The dirty but comfortable curls hung to the floorboards and over the rusty springs.

Fat, hands in pockets, grinning, Wade worked his way down the street, careful to keep in shadow. He knew the Indians could see him, the wet shirt and trousers white. He stayed in the dark. For a time he sat, a drunk rolled in a corner, on an empty porch of the provisional store, resting. He saw a tin can blown suddenly into the air. The sharp-mouthed Indians leapt across the street to the sound of beating drums. He chuckled quietly from deep beneath his leather belt, watched them burn down, tormented by the moon.

Wade again crept lumbering toward the hut on wheels. The thin stick of the chimney turned a spotted orange. In a row of gray false fronts, among a few gilt lettered windows—a town laid out and staged with a few hundred people on the plains—the red wagon took its crooked place like a bloody thorn, an impudent shambles in the midst of cattle houses. It had not been driven to the side but blocked the road.

Wade, abstractly picking a tooth, saw the squaws clustered about the doll size steps. They looked darkly or, a few old and with toothless gums, happily, up to the bright light burning through splits and knotholes in the rain warped door. In the pack he saw one, two, that were maidens in unbelted dresses. The paralytic old chief's sparkler flashed on their tightly drawn black hair. It was a circle he could not enter, never touch those with woodsmoke under their fingernails. The months of the maiden Indians came with the tearing of young dogs; Wade scratched his neck and looked at the gently stooping shoulders.

Suddenly, as bright lips parted, the stolid door flew open. In the heat of the boiling pot stove Cap Leech stood above them, holding by the throat a brown chested boy, the other hand dripping an instrument of metal.

Cap Leech dropped him. The boy—until that one moment the men outside had cried in his stead, he had curled his tongue and perspired—fell in pain from the platform. But Wade, as well as the audience of women, saw that he had jumped. And when he hit the ground he glanced quickly at foster mothers, sisters, clutched his jaw and screamed. The women babbled and turned away. Cap Leech raised the metal, flicked it, and the small skin wrapped molar landed among them. Dismayed, they fought for it, picked it up.

The street was empty except for the fiery Cap Leech still framed in the midget doorway and Wade trembling at his feet. A last string of firecrackers rattled and died. The little man with bare arms did not move.

"What do you want?"

His voice was hoarse from long speechless months. He wore black trousers and a stained vest folded low on a thin scarred waist. He stood with his back baking toward the stove the color of which, a cool glow, increased minute by minute. Glancing at the lantern, "Put it out," he said. Wade sank down and grunted.

Cap Leech did not watch him lay his head on its side, burn his nose, blow, and blow again. With eyes bleakly commanding up and down the street as if the Indians still congregated, he continued merely to wipe, almost polish, the hammer pliers shape of metal. The duster-sized piece of waste rag fluffed up and down as he worked with thin fast fingers. Then, done looking at the town, he flung the tool backward, not turning to aim, and shoved the rag into his hip pocket. The pincers crashed behind the stove.

"It was the Sheriff told me to come over," said Wade and brushed at the soot streaks on his trousers.

Cap Leech stepped into the flames and slammed the door. Wade listened to the hurried sounds, the clattering of small objects, a ransacked scuffling. After a pause he heard the whisper of iron, the shooting of grated coal, and the sudden breathing of the fire. Leech reappeared from beneath the wagon, scowled, flung up the steps and fastened a padlock through the rings.

"Bring that lantern," he said.

He sank into the sheepskin and pushed the stiff, long handled brake. Wade saw that on his feet he wore only a toe curled pair of bedroom slippers.

With the easing forward of the hickory lever and the release of the wooden grip which bound the wheels and which, on wallowing hills, was apt to lock and pitch the wagon into the limbs of a bare tree, smoke flattened from the pipe and the men leaned backward, pulled with the head down charge of a blind horse chased by fire. The driver held a loose rein, ran his other hand through the shedding yellow locks on the seat and, shaggy toes pointed restfully together, stared with eyes that never watered toward the horizon, above and beyond any obstacle that might have crossed their path. The son of a light boned suffragette, kept alive by a spirit half stimulant, half sleep, he bounced unconscious of the twisting wagon frame, the knocks of the makeshift caisson.

"Turn around! Turn around, you've passed it."

"Whoa," said Cap Leech, sending not a signal down the reins, and the horse stopped. An obedient, angular wrenching of the shafts, a tilt as one wheel skidded up and across the sidewalk planking, and again Wade's damp wavy hair scratched in his eyes. The stove at their backs was fanned by speed, not wind, and occasionally, without noise, chunked airy wads of ember from the funnel topped chimney, fireballs that floated in the wake of the blood letter.

The ministerial tie strings, knotted, but no longer in a bow, the high collar flapping about the neck, the ease with which he overrode the country familiar or not, all marked a man who had been anesthetized, against whose chest villagers of fifty years had spit their brains.

He drove with the one hand uselessly extended and peered far ahead of the low stars, dismissed without thinking Clare's shut houses. He would travel unlighted roads to reach the distant end of the river, the last of his line. Echoing moans met him at the limits of every township.

Cap Leech did not stop his horse—wide at the rump it tapered to the small head, jet black prehistoric animal that could run forever —before the jail, but turned it instead, with a whisper to the pinned down ears, between the stone wall and vacant wooden wall. He discovered, without an extra movement, the still and littered end of Clare. The wheels rocked in the glassy sand, the horse exhaled.

"You give me a ride here," said Wade. Leech nimbly disappeared on the other side of the wagon. The silent flatlands, the lonely shrub, the plains, moved in upon the town and passed across the weeded railroad line carrying part of Clare off into the night, a few hundred yards into what was once grazing country, now shorn, beyond which there was nothing. Behind, on the streets they had just left, the loping body of a wild dog appeared at the cloudless, hardly sleeping skyline, turned and bounded into the jail.

"I'll tell you what it says." The Sheriff glanced at Wade, looked at Cap Leech from the side of his eye, wrinkled, brown, a mole. "Put his bag in the corner." But for a moment longer he read to himself, holding with both hands the thumb-pressed pages of the yellow paper book. The thick dry lips hung loose, dissociated from the mind that had been concentrating for a long while and in a bad light. "The new of the moon is best," he said briefly and was again silent. To study, he needed the rough cut desk, gum, dust, and streaks of coal dark ink under his fingers. He was gathered over the printed sheet, deciphering sign by sign, breathing at the end of every sentence. Now and then he stopped and his eyes retraced slowly to the top of the page.

"Why don't you let Wade there take your bag?"

But the zodiac was strong and he fell once more to creasing the paper against the round of his knee, tongue tip appearing at the corner of his mouth. He considered the indoor gardener's calendar, a timetable of work, failure, and church holidays, with a slow beating of his heart and patient, slight movements in the cane chair. A gambled harvest, the weather, and days on which accidents were most likely to occur, he calculated; and he discovered, prodding the elements, that they were in the old of the moon. He shut it, leaned forward, and carefully lay it before him on sheets scrawled with dates of years long past and those still to come.

"Wade," staring at Cap Leech, "go bring me that pointing dog. She shouldn't be out back."

The Sheriff stretched forth a palm like a large gland, then Leech; and they shook hands in the last quarter, some few hours after the Minnesota medicine man, hardly planning to pause, had entered Clare. And, having allowed the Sheriff to grasp his own quick fingers —despite lotions of disinfectants and the protection of rubber gloves in the past they were covered with growths of small warts—Cap Leech placed his black satchel on the desk between them, snapped it open. The odor of herbs and germicides, a sharp perfume, rose among the smells of leather and tarnished handcuffs. One smell was strongest, living faintly upon the body of the man with the small bag. Leech pushed up the dirty rolls of his sleeves—nothing tied concealed to that gray flesh—and, reaching into the satchel, brought forth a small tin can and placed it also on the desk. The can and a few pieces of metal were all that remained of the Leech who in his youth had stood thin, well washed, and stern before the cadaver of an aged negro.

Ether. It lay in the bottom of the can like turpentine. The Sheriff bowed slowly forward, sniffed once, twice. He breathed such fumes never before found floating in the far-country kitchens. But, foreign as they were even to the Sheriff, they were fumes that vaguely suggested the fractured leg, were tainted with the going under or coming out of a whimpering sleep. His head nodded. Then the Sheriff straightened and, fumbling with the blade of a little knife, cut at the insides of an apple-large cob pipe. It filled his hand, was covered with kernelless pock holes, missing teeth. He puffed quickly and the sweet fumes disappeared in tobacco smoke.

"You use that on them, then," said the Sheriff.

"Sometimes," answered Leech, "sometimes I don't."

"It's in your clothes." The Clare Sheriff was invested with the office to inspect, whip, or detain any unique descendant of the fork country pale families, was in a position to remember when they settled and how well or poorly they had grown. But before him stood a man concerned even more than himself with noxious growth, who was allowed, obviously schooled, to approach his fellow men with the intimate puncture of a needle.

"Why don't you sit down?" said the Sheriff. Now and then he still caught a taste, some sort of chloride or oxide, at least a poison, of the medicine man's evaporating drug. "What else you got in that bag?" He picked up his pamphlet, licked his thumb, then with a

42

sweep cleared the smothered desk. "You fellows have it all," he said in a friendly, uncertain voice to the stranger who, sixty himself, might have been discovered plucking under the chin an old man suffering a head cold. "Hurt them when you want to, collecting all those bottles and knives. But," and the Sheriff looked to the door, "there's not much doctoring or tooth pulling for you here."

"That so."

"I don't believe there's a tree standing within a hundred mile where you could hang a shingle. If there was, they'd tear it down."

Cap Leech lifted the tin can, sniffed, fixed the cotton stopper. Those eye whites, dull bits of glass pressed against the skin, hovered over the floor. Without raising them he began to laugh, "Open your hand." Slowly, in the fat of the Sheriff's upturned palm, he drew a circle with his broken fingertip. "Disease," he said, "thriving. Catch a fly in your fist and you could infect the town." Quickly, with the iced cotton, he swabbed the hand, let it go. "Clean. For awhile."

"Wade," the Sheriff drew back and called, "come here, Wade!"

In a stoop Wade pulled the pointer through the doorway. It brought with it the smell of rain, the smell of paws, forelegs and chest soaked in storm and caked with the mud of a downpour; it twisted its head, drops beating against its eyes, and shook, would have spattered the walls, between Wade's knees. All day it shied and staggered under the sun. But by nightfall it was able to force moisture, to yelp at the shell-like roll of a cloudburst in its ears, to walk as if leaving puddles across the floor, to smell as if the rain had actually come down and driven it bleating and thin into a rivulet filling ditch.

Wade walked stiff-legged, raised his head to smile, and pulled, lifted the dog by its throat. All four of the animal's legs were rigid, hind legs clamped straight up and down, front paws crossed over its bleeding snout. He dropped the dog in the middle of the room, re-leased the matted fur. His hands were wet, the bottoms of his trousers damp.

"Sheriff, this dog is scratched."

"Scratched?"

"Yes, sir. She's cut up."

"Got ahold of her, did they?"

"Yes, sir. They must have claws."

The first motorcycle the Sheriff saw appeared at dusk, bounded around a corner of the granary and sped without lights down one gutter of the sanded street. He had raised a hand against it, started at the whirr of wheels spoked with dirt and a few oily flower stems, and had begun to run clumsily, freshly shaved and scented, as it jumped the wooden walk, leapt, a small thunderbird, and flashed through a plate glass window.

The Sheriff sat down, stared thoughtfully at the animal whose rump still clung to the air, whose injured nose lay hidden. Then, slowly, he reached for it, lifted it with a brief grunt until its chest was on his lap. And he waited until the nose was uncovered, while it probed blindly, and at last allowed his fat cheek to be licked, touched with blood. He chuckled, "She's been out back."

After shoving and kissing the round face of the Sheriff—the tongue that was clamped between its own teeth flicked once the lobe of his ear—the slick keen head of the pointer dropped and with slow high climbing motions the dog stepped and pawed ungainly hind legs against his trousers, attempted to thrust and double its whole body onto his knees. The Sheriff held his breath, slowly pushed the pointer to the floor.

Without a murmur it slunk off. "She's sick," said the Sheriff and watched for some expression to curl across the healer's cleft face. Not

44

a grimace appeared, but slowly, with slackening pulse, he seemed to unwind and, reaching once more the tin can for a whiff of salts, dropped a white hand tolerantly to the desk top. There was a switch up his spine, a spark of truth in the watery tapping of his fingers. "Don't say anything," the Sheriff stepped forward, then behind the desk, "I'll do the talking." He rubbed the prognosticator's pamphlet against his beard. "He'll listen," thought the Sheriff, "no traveling man's that good."

Beyond them bloomed the desert that had starved to silence the calls of loveless dogs, buried under successive sand waves the hoof prints of single fading riders or the footprints of man and woman running with clothes bundled quickly beneath their arms. Any no-mad tribes that had once burned raiding fires at night were gone, human drops sprinkled and spent in the sand, as bodies slipped from the edge of the horse blanket, had been settled upon and obscured by wingless insects or fried, like the heads of small but ruddy desert flowers, in the sun of one afternoon.

"I said," stuffing a fistful of tobacco over the white ash in the bottom of the pipe, "there's just one man who died out here. Only the one death that come to anything. For ten, even twelve years, in all that time there ain't been a single robber shot in the head, no rancher fatally struck by snakes. It hasn't been long enough for any man to grow old enough to die . . ."

The jail, with its door standing open and another locked, kept all men who spit or talked within its walls comfortable on gray lead painted floor or dry cane, confidential, close, by its very smell and heat of confinement, preserved them amidst the circles of the desert. No sound passed between the padlock and smoky boulder. The scratching of infected toes, the whispering from swollen, hair covered throats, died near the foundations of the jail. Away, no voice called for help, the desert might have sunk from sight, beyond detection and points of the compass.

Only the soft voice croaking full of stories and the listener, at that hour, feeling just old enough to wait. The Sheriff looked up and down the page, turned, flipped another one and paused. *"Aquarius is poor,"* he said and thought, "That will hold him, ain't a chemical sounds that good to the ear." He added, *"Sagittarius is poor,* also."

The purveyor of menthol, iodine, and peppermint stepped to the window as the drone continued. There were no dark house fronts, no flashing signs. Only the dented black plains stretched from the window to the horizon without a flicker of movement except for a shadow that now and then crossed the buzzing screen. For a long while Cap Leech stood pressed against the wall, listening. He looked toward the cow country for some speck of a herd against the night sky or a lone rider nodding over the pommel. The mosquitoes ticked against the screen in his face.

The Sheriff scowled into the magic page. *"Trim no trees or vines when the Moon or Earth is in Leo. For they will surely die."* He stopped reading, marked his place, and began to talk.

It is a lawless country.

In the beginning, before the sights were even taken for Mistletoe, Government City, before the women and children arrived, when stray cows could stop wherever they pleased below the high ground to water, and the water in its turn could slug downstream to flood, when the nearest city, not including Clare which was only a post on the plain, was over the line into the next state—at that time, as winter came on and workers migrated to the project anyway, upon the whole head of the bluff there was founded a colony of a thousand tents that smoked like an Indian village through the hard snow. Ten or twenty men to a tent, they penny-anted by lantern light and only came out into the falling snow to watch when a load of shovels arrived or the crated yellow tractor was slid from the rear of a truck and left in a shallow dune to await spring. For days the men tramped out in small groups to lean over, and touch, and inspect the box of spare parts that someone had struck open with an iron bar. The temperature went down.

There were no streets and hardly a pathway, no community hall or cookhouse; fires were built before each tent and the tin cans, thrown behind one, landed in the dooryard of the next and slid beneath the snow. A ton of steel cable was finally shipped in and remained a solid mountain for the winter. In hours when the snowfall ceased and the eye could travel far over the white flatlands, the new workers would creep from the tents and standing on the bluff in the wind, look down upon the widening overflow, the ice blocked river. New sheepskin coated friends were made in these lulls on the ridge.

Men landed in camp all through the months of sleet and snow. Tents trickled down the slope, clustered in pockets and mushroomed in four or five protected holes in the land. Fat Chance, Reshuffle, Dynamite, they were unrecorded towns still remembered by a few in Gov City.

The storms tossed heavier than ever on Christmas, the river was out of sight and only the explosions of the ice told them it was there below. Tent flaps were staked down, the cans burning a skim of gasoline covered them all with soot. Hardly a worker dared face the gales that out of the northern moose country turned and vaulted in the hail swept bowl; nor would they walk far on the cornerless white range. But one old driller, stumbling a few yards from his place in the circle, carrying a shovel and wad of excelsior, discovered, in a dry notch of stone and sand, a short green frozen twig of pine. He nailed it to the ridgepole. And grinning down at the men, shaking his beard that was still black, he threw the shovel into its public corner and pointed upward.

"That there's Mistletoe!" he cried.

When it finally thawed and the river rose, when the mud sloshed over the top of their boots and shoepacks, the women came. From that time on the wash was hung to dry out of doors. In the sun— when it was warm and a fresh breeze rose from the receding banks—

in mid-morning, whole lines of workmen hunched forward on crates or squatted in the sand and earth that was still damp, with dirty towels on their shoulders, not turning to talk, staring off where birds were flying or hills emerging from the prairie, getting haircuts from their wives.

As the tide was stopped and in the dry season the river, at its weakest, was pinched off, the old bed became a flat of seepage and puddles of dead water. When the men turned the tideland into a ship-yard, built barges and could swarm from one bank to the other, poles and lines were raised and Gov City finally telegraphed to Clare.

"There isn't any town out here."

"Sure there is," said Camper to his wife, "not so small either, if I can find it." He braced the fluid steering wheel against his stomach, squinted at the enormous thorny balls of sage that rolled in slow motion before the headlights.

"You're dreaming again. No one's dumb enough to put a town out here. Take us back to the highway."

Sharp lifeless blades of prairie grass scratched at the undersides of the automobile, crackled to the slow turning of the tires. The armored vehicle with its veils of glass, shrouded in blunt searching beams of light and swinging, dipping its useless aerial in the hot air, prowled forward toward the unknown dried out river, now and then dropping its front bumper into a mound of sand. Camper pressed, released the accelerator with his sandaled foot, watched for signs of a track not wholly lost, saw only the yellow powder, the needles of a still and tangled earth. He felt that the inflated rubber of his car wheels must be crushing colonies of red ants, crazed lizards, bugs caught before they had time to hum and fly. He sat on the edge of the padded leather seat.

"What's the matter with you? Turn around!"

"Only a minute now, Lou, you'll see. A real town, I know it."

"You can't kid me. You just want a chance to use that tent. I'll sleep in the car."

He could not find it. Once he stopped the automobile—all its wide tapering body listed—and climbed out, leaving the door open, its sharp edge jammed in the sand. He looked back to the sound of the heavy engine on weeded soil, to the small light burning over the blue blouse, the green silk slacks of the woman. Then, bent double, he stepped in front of the headlights and peered closely at a few square feet of ground, looking for some trace of a house, a piece of wood once shaped by saw, a brick that had burned under the fire of a kiln; as if he expected to find the town or its remnants in a hole at his feet. The cowboy had spoken of it, he himself remembered it and yet, picking up a handful of grit and dust, perhaps she was right.

"I don't see it," he said. The bites itched on his chest and shoulders.

"I could tell from the highway," his wife answered. "There weren't any signs."

Though not stopped by barrier—fence, rock or ravine—the automobile was sucked close to the loose and dibbled earth, slowed by the invisible roots of parasite plants stretched like strings across its path, exhausted of speed and air. Camper felt a harsh and lazy magnetism that, foot by foot, might crack its windows, strip it of paint and draw the stuffing from the seats. He watched for something to steer by.

"You can't expect to find a town just anywhere," said his wife.

And at that moment they were attacked for the second time during the night by snakes. They ran over it. Flat and elongated, driven upon in sleep, it wheeled, rattling from fangs to tail, chased them, caught up with the car, slithered beneath it, raced ahead into the light and reared. The snake tottered, seemed to bounce when it became blind, and, as Camper touched the brake, lunged so that it appeared to have shoulders, smashed its flat pear skull against the solid, curved glass of one headlamp, piercing, thrusting to put out the light.

"Go back and kill it! Go on, get out of this car!"

Quickly he drove ahead, reaching one hand through the darkness to quiet her, and saw, hardly above the sands, the railless, short rotten planks of an abandoned sidewalk starting from the desert.

"I told you, I knew she was still here!"

Lou put her forehead against the glass.

She lifted the boy into his left arm, piled his right with towels. In a free hand he clutched the cowhide suitcase.

"There's nobody here," she hissed as they climbed the boot smooth dormitory steps. The rooms, down segregated corridors, were dark, not a light nor single man appeared in the foyer on the walls of which hung pictures—a girl, a horse's head—torn from magazines. Standing together for a moment on the cold linoleum floor, Camper imagined forty bearded shovelers and forty china mugs stretched along the bare planks of a makeshift table: a silent, before dawn meal.

The soft, fibreboard walls of the corridor sagged, split at the bottoms. Sand swept across the floor. Camper padded forward, stopped, moved again in his extra wide, sea rotted sandals; behind him the red high heels of the woman cracked.

"Try that one, Lou," he whispered, and in a narrow room, screen half ripped from the window, they looked upon a tousled iron bed, a body that slept beneath a raincoat.

"Here," he said, "try '22'." The number was splashed on the door in peeling whitewash.

"Open it yourself!"

Camper squeezed the rattling glass knob between his fingers, pushed, shielded by all he carried, leaned into the dust and mold. "No," he whispered, staring a moment, "not this one, either."

The lamp, beside a card table with a hole ripped in its center, worked, but the lock catch dangled from the door jamb.

"Keep the shades down," he told her after each trip to the car, "there's no sense letting everyone know we're here."

"Everyone! You got a nerve." She sat on a campstool, stretched herself, blew down the front of her blouse. As soon as Camper had set up the cots and slipped the small revolver under one pillow, settled the boy in his mother's bed and untangled the mosquito netting, he stooped and plied quickly, methodically, through his own valise. He removed the delicate rod, the clock-like reel, the green and yellow dun flies.

"The best fishing in the world is right here, Lou," he mumbled and collected the bright and pointed gear.

She stood up, wet with silk. "You think I'll swallow that? You got eyes, you've driven across it as well as me. After five hundred miles they wouldn't dump garbage on and not a spot to get a drink in, you think I'm going to believe there's water in this place? Let alone a fish!" She watched him pin the flies to his flowing collar, stick the collapsed rod in a pocket above his wide and boneless hip. She considered the smile on his face, the flipping hands.

Suddenly she rose still higher, spit, shouted after him down the rank and hollow hall: "You dirty little dog," laughing, trembling at her own intuition, "you been here before!"

She was alone. She listened, pulled the sheet across the boy, went immediately to the window and raised the shade. And, breasts half thrust, half fallen against the screen, she found herself unable to move as she stared into a watchful, silent figure pressed close to the other side.

The creature continued to watch. It was made of leather. Straps, black buckles and breathing hose filled out a face as small as hers, stripped of hair and bound tightly in alligator skin. It was constructed as a baseball, bound about a small core of rubber. The driving goggles poked up from the shiny cork top and a pair of smoked glasses fastened in the leather gave it malevolent and overflowing eyes. There was a snapped flap on one side that hid an orifice drilled for earphones. Its snout was pressed against the screen, pushing a small bulge into the room.

The snout began to move. It poked without sight toward the flattened slippery flesh of Camper's wife. And with that first sound of scraping she turned her back, swayed, stepped quickly from the room.

There were men, perhaps women, in the building who, thought Camper's wife, still confiscated fatback and a few blunt tools from local ordinance and who, despite buck tooth, caved chin, lockjaw and blisters still existed, warped and blackened in the wake of the caterpillar and dusty mare. As she walked away from her own door left ajar, she heard the wriggling of their toes, put her ear against the walls, softly knocked. She sniffed for the spot where Camper himself, years before, had squinted through the screens or rolled asleep. With crimping fingers she tucked the bottom of her blouse into the slacks.

"He won't catch anything," she thought.

A light burned in the kitchen. She stood on the threshold and watched as an old woman, after setting a pie tin before one of two men at the table and opening the stove on the coals, grunted, smiled, lifted heavy blue skirts and tucked a dollar bill, closely folded, into the top of a fattened snow white stocking.

"Sit down," said Harry Bohn to the Finn, "I ain't done dinner."

"I'm going home."

"Sit down." Bohn began the pie and the crippled Finn, knocking a chair free of the table with one of his fluttering canes, sat on the edge of it, braces grinding, and watched him chew. Lou saw that the cook, Norwegian, fat, expected the whole pie to be eaten, saw that the small man, fidgeting, wore no clothes except his airy overalls. He was slight, wrapped around by the thinness tight upon a body that had lost weight never to regain it. His white canes tapped constantly, he drummed them as another might his fingertips.

"You wouldn't run off on me, would you, Finn?"

"I got things. Lots of things to do, Bohn." The top of his overalls flared stiffly from the middle of his back, one broad strap and brass button slipped from a shoulder, pinched, transparent. "So I can't sit around with you," snapped the lightweight ex-bronc rider, who in the beginning had ridden from many chutes with spurs entangled high on an animal's withers.

"Tonight," Bohn leaned back, his lips bubbled, "you're going to."

He saw the woman in the doorway. His mouth fell open—blue mash, blue gums and teeth—he saw her stare, he frowned and put his hands on the table as if to rise. "Yes, sir," fingers sprung without thought into a fist, eyes back to the Finn, "we don't get around it. You ain't going to move, unless I say." And the cook behind him, leaning between his needs, his body, and the fire, licking her lips as he, nodding before he spoke, looked at the same time toward the doorway and shook her silver braids, spoke to Camper's wife.

"No supper. You're too late."

"That's right," Bohn's eyes in the plate, hiding the mouth with the back of his hand, "kitchen's closed."

For Lou his mouth was open, his chin still sagged. The berries, the purple fish roe, still hung in the air and filled a vanished face; she saw a crawling, half digested bunch of grapes, a birthmark—at a single mouthful—swelling into sight between his lips. Bohn never looked at her again.

He had an old man's kidney. He had an old man's tumorous girth and thickly dying wind, a hardening on the surface of his armpits. Chest and shoulders were solidified against youth, bulged in what he assumed to be the paunch of middle age; he was strapping, suffered a neuralgia in winter, a painful unlimbering in the spring. A few fingers were broken, snubbed, since an old man labors from stone to knife to saw to possible tractor accident and back to the single burning of a match flame short in argument. He could laugh, sparsely, at the exploits of men over fifty who enacted, he believed, all they claimed; his own prowess, he told them, had been struck off, like a head of hair, by maturity. And he was, except for a few patches that had to be shaved monthly by a barber, bald; lost by pernicious exposure to the sun, kept from water and finally pulled out one night in a troubled sleep by bloody, rasping fingertips. He mimicked, with unclean, pyretic dignity, the limp folds under the chin, the cockles in the cheeks, the gasp of wisdom and inflammation, the rock-like, seasoned cough of the prime, half invalided buck.

Bohn argued at, commanded his world and saw it under the pale of bitter years when imaginary friends die off. From this weathered mask and within this swollen body of whore-wounded time—he was thirty years old—skipped eyes blue and lively, curious for abuse, soured at the sight of visiting women passing close and strange among the undershirts, the beards of the members of his town.

"Thegna's finished for the day, pooed over all the cabbage you care to, ain't you, Thegna?" And now and then, instead of speaking to or looking at the mustang buster, he thrust an arm across the table, struck the wood to keep the small man in his place. "You loved the boys already, ain't you, Thegna?" The one arm on her waist, the other, just out of reach, aiming at the Finn, "In Fat Chance worried all of us at once."

Lou looked quickly at the small but rotund cook.

Bohn broke away. He stood up and immediately, with a clatter of sticks, the frail, the chronically thin ex-rider left the table.

Bohn stopped in the doorway and whispered once more to the trussed and stocky, water-eyed and trembling woman. "Thegna, did you pull on your big hip boots when the dam slid in?"

She nodded, back against the stove, and continued to bow up and down her flushed and weeping head. The apron shot up in warm and baffled flight.

"Thegna here will learn you," he said as he quickly passed the flash of blue-green silk.

Lou escaped the flaying of the tumbling canes.

He shied, big and halting as he was, at the web texture of the flyless slacks and at the emerald apparatus that lived and breathed, but further at the metal relic buried in the middle of her chest, visible, through the silk, in its modest wedge. At that time it was the only cross in Mistletoe, Lou the only woman despite several who gathered in the cook's room for cards.

Below the window and under the stare of searchlights brilliant atop dry and root choked posts, a file of creaking men sat still the length of the dormitory wall. Their backs were encrusted to the glittering tar board and they could not stir, singly mushroomed in a row, did not twist white and curious faces toward the upstairs window at the sound of women, the exchange, starting overhead, of far carrying tones and smiles. The sound was enough, was robbed of sweetness near the ground by the chemically white light and itching in their feet; by the guitar that was struck now and then shortly above the rattling of the pails, crouched upon by the player who sang, suddenly muffled, as a man talking to himself and not in serenade.

Tin helmets at their sides, after a day of clinging to the turbine tower and before bed, they stilled the creeping of the fungus across their feet by immersion, waved them automatically, spreading the toes, in the medicinal, violet fluid that filled the pails. Septic patches of flaking skin and trails of the discharge from the soles of their feet caked the bottoms of their shoes and in the early morning reimpregnated cooling sores, fired, a sudden yeast, under men's weight on the earth. But at night they rolled their trousers above the knee, sat still. Beyond the crushed glass of the lot they faced and away in the darkness, stretched open snares and painful walks, sand, black brush and the dam. They hung their heads, at night retreated in blue denim and with phosphorescent joints and bones to the gritty wall—and did not, after women slept and from the porch of a store, watch through heavy cobwebbed evenings for a moonrise. The women were awake.

"You better tell me about him," demanded Lou. She leaned at the window and several times, in the beginning, looked down on the black and waxen heads, well lit naked legs, the narrow backs. "Been here before and damned himself. Or had a good time." She glanced down again—searchlights hit her egg blue breast and sparkling cross—and breathed deeply, staring after caterpillars curled on a branch. "He's short." She looked at the gold braids, tarnished, at the cook with canvas hips, and she began to breathe like the fat woman, through her mouth. Already, giggling and without a word, the cook's head shook in denial, admitting no eye on her bosom, no rocks thrown. "He sweats in bed," said Camper's wife. "He can stick things into himself and not feel. If he's mad he cries. Remember?"

The journeying man was followed: a bandog with a trailing chain, by fighters brawling a hundred steps behind, by a fish that escaped in the years before or a woman pointing no sooner had he passed. He stepped fidgeting through the darkness, thinking now and then of the dead man, while, in the body of one and the back-biting of the other, he was described between two women lashed together for the night.

"A blue spot on his chest? Punches you in his sleep? Come on," Lou urged in the foreknowledge of a young girl, "you weren't just cooking all that time." And she played upon the drawstrings of the bag they shared, pledged that dual experience imposed by birth—in its welter all men were innocent—to outlast, roundabout and broad, the lone conception men carried in a joke and for which they fought time and again. "Any other place I wouldn't have missed him," trying to judge the years and deducting pounds accordingly, squinting at the woman's shape of old, "telling me he just come here to fish! He can do that in the bathtub." And the cook stood stolid, no keener than when she had backed against the stove.

Lou flung away her own blonde hair. She slouched, eyes level with the cook's, gained weight, inched like a man to the window where perfume would be safely lost into the salty night. Had she a bandana she would have tied it around her head, blown out her cheeks. She hid her bright fingers in the pockets of her slacks. She swayed, gone white, as if she too had just kissed a mouth thick with pie and tobacco leaves, just come from a man in black blucher shoes and pants swelled with a bladder beneath the belt. "Think," she said, "I want to know. Did he have the nerve?" Then, against the snapping of the guitar and smell of scattered red pepper seeds: "He ran straight to it all right. Like a buried bone!"

Thegna revolved, clapped both hands into crimson cheeks and spun so that the back of her head became as blunt and sealed as her face. Her eyes disappeared, popped in pain—nerves, glitter, fluid—into her head as in laughter an egg or thimble is suddenly swallowed whole and the body continues to shake while vomiting through the nose. In the old days Thegna had fired upon thieving Indians, shot her rifle on the fourth of July and, unarmed, stormed once to the reservation to organize a convention of stercoricolous squaws. She was the first to order a crystal set and the last to give up wearing a money belt. One braid flew loose and clung flatly to her shortened arm's thick end, one breast trailed the other.

"Stop it," hissed Camper's wife, "shut up!"

But the laughter of the cook was dry, the fat goose flurry came in silence and the earth jug color rose, ebbed, beamed from her body, friendless, harmless, a howl on lips too old to part. Without stopping or turning to the door she spoke: "Fatima," words clearly, distinctly extracted from the pounding bulk, "this is the visiting lady. She'll play with us."

Three disappointed women and then a fourth made long-jointed simple gestures toward the chairs they wished to sit in. They smelled of the tedder and handfuls of dry grass. Their heads turned slowly from objects knocked against to the cook, to Camper's wife, moved along a thread of angular, impaired vision with apologetic sidelong sweeps, with shrugs of caution. They took single heavy steps as if the room had been reversed since the night before. Tall, large bones easily injured, deprived of something they were intent upon, not noticing and hardly afraid of the stranger, they fiddled, settled to restlessness somehow conscious of the years it would take them to make friends.

"You sit anywhere, Mrs.," said the cook, "we don't play partners."

And Lou heard a sudden back country blow on metal strings—a hand clapped across the neck of the guitar below—and thought, bitterly hoped, that it might jerk them into the corridors, send them dancing.

A few old couples waltzed. They came from some watering point, perhaps near the hills, or from some dry plot of garden even further away than One Hundred Acres Grassland. Their overalls bagged, buttons flashed, armpits darkened halfway to belts and sashes.

Luke looked them over. He stepped by silent women, by men fanning themselves with wide brimmed hats, and approached the band. The cornet player stood up. Streamers sagged the whole length of the gym, and the raffling wheel, red, yellow and green with rusty nails driven round the hub to catch the tab and pick the winner, was pushed out of the way behind the bandstand, taller than a man.

The two dime collectors at the door in white shirtsleeves and muddy boots, shared a pack of cigarettes and ripped matches across their britches. They began to whistle a song together that their fathers, two buddy muckers, had taught them from Reshuffle days.

"Hey, Luke," two little girls stood out of reach and clutched each other's arms, "where's Mr. Bohn? Where is he, Luke?"

He considered for a moment and then: "Bohn ain't worked his way up this far as yet."

An old man and woman, he in his straw sun hat and she hiding her face in smiles, were urged to keep dancing by scattered applause and the hoots of children.

"Great dance, eh, Luke?"

As the man with moustaches saw Luke stride to the shower stairs, he called, "If Bohn gets here, I'll tell him he needs a good cold washing."

"Much obliged."

Luke switched on the light, cut loose the torrent of water piped directly from the dam, left his boots on the bottom step and catching his breath, soaped and drenched himself. The slippery wooden slats cut into and relieved his itching feet.

The stalls were made of planking from the scaffolds. Black and smooth after years of steaming and under the spray of alkaline soap, uneven in height and thickness, chopped into bath hole walls and darkened by ten years of scrubbers, these boards had been the beams and stanchions of the trestle across the river, had been the ribs and machine marred decks of barges. They were salvaged from long piles on the banks, turned from sea craft to bridge, to tool shed, scrapped and saved. They were never burned. A few long awkward unsinkable beams had been hooked from the still churning water around the catastrophe itself. They survived the Slide, floated and were towed landward to dry. At one time the river was filled with the lattice of new lumber, white sawdust fell on the muddy current and the prairie ranchers, riding out of the dunes and through the tents on the bluff to watch, saw wood come into the sand country and not only cut, but cut to special sizes. They stole it until guards mounted on the piles. Then they joined the crews to be near it.

The walls of the shower stalls were rough above the shoulder line from hobnail boots and still bore the deep impression of the chains. The spike holes were large enough to peer through. Meetings were made in the showers, began or ended there in the roar of midnight waters behind soaked green trenchcoats hung across the openings. The waste troughs under the floor slats were caked white and year after year pieces of soap, fallen through the bars, clogged the wired drains, turned thick and dissolved.

Luke washed under his arms, hunching forward to keep his hat and cigarette out of the wild stream, stuck one leg and then the other into the spray and hopped out, shaking, cold, standing on his toes as if he still wore high heels. He hurried to the stairway, a white bowlegged ranger dressed down to the neck and was dry before the shirt, pants and boots were pulled from the heap. He swung shut the iron wheel of the valve and heard the many damp closets dripping in the darkness.

He reached the landing of the stairs in time to hear the shooting, to see the musicians jump and the old men slam the women out of the way. He heard the grinding of the tires, the squawk of mudguard mounted horns, the scraping of the rider's boots steadying their machines. One of the dime collectors appeared in the doorway.

"Do they come in or not?"

They listened and some peered into the darkness beyond. They could see only the other dime collector watching his feet. Luke climbed to the bandstand. Some went to one side of the room, a few to the other. Luke counted the hands.

By a terrible application of brakes and a violent twisting of accelerators, the heavy engined motorcycles ground into a tight, whirling, dust-churning circle in the center of the street as the drivers threw down one heel and lay the machines on their sides, jerkined Indians. They made three revolutions, knocking stones against the gymnasium walls. The Red Devils worked and struggled in their glistening saddles to brake and then explode the engines as the silver ornaments, the enormous taillamps, the sleek black gas tanks ending in their crotches blazed in the light from the doorway. Their gauntlets grasped and pulled on the widespread steel horns.

Several of the light cycles were doubly ridden but in the speed, the smoke, the clamor, it was impossible to tell which were men and which women. At the end of the last circle the lead machine and its small tightly belted driver cut off in a straight line toward the south and in a thin, flashing column the Red Devils disappeared into the black country and the exhaust flares clipped out one by one.

The raised windows and grates rattled for a moment with the sudden, unpleasant chock and starting of engines and the band began to play.

"They had jewels all over them," said the boy.

Luke wiped his face, throat and upper chest with his neckerchief. "We don't want to hear about it," he said.

no one wants to hear what I got to say," said Ma.

Day or night could not be measured by what she did or the way she dressed. Her bedding on the floor was always open and roughed as if she had just climbed wearily from it or was about to lay herself down again for a moment's uneasy rest. She napped all through the night. The sun might be breaking or clouding over as she stood at the stove changing her dressing, reaching for the roll of bandage between the red bottle and pepper tin, peering at her forearm sore by the light of the coals. She stood on a little patch of carpet before the stove summer or winter, in the early evening or the long middle breath of the night, and wore her stocking cap and slippers, daytime dress and high socks.

"My sore's been ailing me again," she said.

Ma had been outlying Gov City for ten remembered years, her cooking chimney seen always smoking, a Lampson marketing for her and talking about her every week, but no one knew when or how the sore had sprung upon her arm. Because of the vermin in the chicken wings, or some recurrent bone breath in the victuals, or some flowering growth cropped up in the slough of the river bed, it never healed but gave her trouble when she stirred or rolled over. She tended it with the same frown and preoccupation as possessed the cowboy when he lanced or cauterized the discolored wound of a pit viper.

"You give it to me," and she half turned to the Mandan to let her see. The girl sat reading a catalogue with breasts lunged against the table, oil gleaming on her black hair and spotting the red wool sweater. She licked her fingers and slowly turned the page to another smeared picture of an accordion.

"Mulge never would have let me be this way," said Ma.

The mile long knoll of his grave mound was an incomplete mountain, a pile of new earth erupted between the bluffs, a patch, a lighter hue of brown, across the river road. It was a shoveler's mission, the largest heap of dirt and the longest tomb of any channel impediment from the trickling source of the trouble to its mouth on the distant gulf. They had stripped the topsoil of the basin, picked at the surface and weeds, uncovered the shifting red clay for acres and finally, in the last stages of the project, been stopped at the yellow peakless rise itself. Not that they had been able to move the mountain into place and rear it foot by foot, but rather they had been unable to tear it down and had merely left it, defaced of former cliffs and ridges, and without a name. It took Luke's seeding badly; it remained undisguised and visitors looked vainly for the excavations from which it must have come.

A few tool sheds remained below the dam. Rust-colored, barely overgrown cuts still lay along the lower banks, but the enormous center of the channel, from which the mountain had been pumped and drawn, had resumed one night its listless flat shape. It shifted as before when under water, but in currents and directions that could be recorded only on the seismograph by magnetic flux and by the wary, almost invisible nestings and flights of insects from one drift of remaining dead water to the next.

It was a sarcophagus of mud. It filled the gap between two lesser hills and prevented, by raising spit and shoals to sight, the flag flying traffic of river boats where a few had glittered in the night and crawled before. The dam caused to be beached the homemade leaking skiffs of ranchers whose land backed up to the mud colored misty fathoms trailing seaward. Where once bleak needles and spines had popped crookedly from the banks and a few flowers increasingly withered into the plain and disappeared, only the dust from the southward slope, swirling into the air, and a few animal bones and tin cans from a still deeper generation, survived. One small city of the plain lasted to welcome the tourist trade and issue reports on the depth of the almost foreign, dark pan of water. And yet, from the construction yard diggings, from the bits of wire in the sand and a beer bottle that might be found instead of a wreath, inscription, or shredded flag on the graded fresh slope of earth, from the drippings that seethed out of its dark insides and were measured, it seemed that the luck of gamblers, engineers and women had appeared, and from the bare mound indistinguishable from the bluffs at dusk, the highways, planned townsites and rock formations pushing west had stopped, fossilized and emerged.

It moved. The needles, cylinder and ink lines blurring on the heat smeared graph in the slight shade of evening, tended by the old watchman in the power house, detected a creeping, downstream motion in the dam. Leaned against by the weight of water, it was pushing southward on a calendar of branding, brushfires and centuries to come, toward the gulf. Visitors hung their mouths and would not believe, and yet the hill eased down the rotting shale a beetle's leg each several anniversaries, the pride of the men of Gov City who would have to move fast to keep up with it. But if this same machine, teletyping the journey into town, was turned upon the fields, the dry range, the badlands themselves, the same trembling and worry would perhaps be seen in the point of the hapless needle, the same discouraging pulse encountered, the flux, the same activity. It might measure the extinction of the snake or a dry finger widening in erosion.

They smoothed it with a shovel. They thrived in the shadow of the dam but kept to the bottom of the mound. Only the cowboy trod upon its sweltering slope above his kin, only small parties of electricians dragged their wires on its baking crest. Few took the top road. They could see it from their horseshoe windows but rarely climbed it, unlike the tourists who arrived each week in season, labored over the trackless dirt, not steep but long, gauging upon it little prints that would evaporate by dusk, to stand panting for a moment, cover their heads with handkerchiefs and say: "I had an uncle had a farm out there. Used to graze under them miles of water."

If the employment of dredge and suction pump had done little toward changing the contour and imperfections of an already dry south, it had done nothing to the land northward but submerged it— havoc was hardly tossed upon a natural sea bottom. The outriders on a Sunday fished over the old barn. The current swelled upon pasture, receded from field, sinking or skirting raised sandstone islands or covered dunes with a virgin darkness. And it barely washed the sand and granite sea side of the dam. It held. They told the visitors that it would.

They spoke of it as dry land. But the land they chose to walk upon had never been scooped out by caterpillar nor been flung showering, fine as grain, from spades. Shapeless in the darkness, they never watched it when in their cars parked on roadless, adjoining bluffs, and more certainly, never watched the moon from blankets spread across the crest. But of its own accord and from its own weight fissures appeared and deceptively closed, trapping wrestling mice and young lizards. By them the whole ten years of work must someday crack apart one dry season, and sift away like earth pitched against a screen.

No one saw the Gov City man shoveled under. He died at the drop of a lash, was noticeably absent only after a count of heads. The lip of new pumped clay melted with the downward breath of an elevator through its shaft, left the end of the trestle and the steam engine atop it swaying loosely and cataclysmic for a moment, vertical beams dripping small pebbles and slime. Then, as the structure snapped with a minimum of screeching timber, it carried the catafalque, its joints of wood and forward-most portions of the bridge of skill, into the hollow hand and to the bottom. Two weeks of scaffold were rebuilt and another donkey engine ordered from the yards. Advancing slowly, testing each step with a gentle, forward foot—but the sound was gone, the earth firm again—they reached, one by one, the crest of disaster, a wide settled trough of mud barely higher than the freshly, nakedly drained original bed. And though they searched and tried to remember, the incalculable loss of small tools could not be reckoned. They were called back to solid ground by an engineer's whistle blowing from the bluff, and the sound of low lapping water followed them from the scene of such toil, from the miasmal landscape.

Tent after tent in Mistletoe collapsed, canvas sides sprawled in the sand, ridge poles cracked and, as shock clouds passed dryly over the rope-marked streets, rumors rose, subsided, and the town got drunk. Though the lid of the portmanteau had dropped and no one knew what was lain away, packed just under the eye of the town, though there was nothing to do but pump, shovel, raise up the earth and grade, "Squashed, that's what he was," said many and disorder grew. "By now, he's slid into China," and coolies cried above the dam, rolling it with boulders, while a country that was thought to go no further than the sea, went down.

Thegna cried the loudest. She caught the spirit of the Slide in sawed-off gum boots, canvas gloves and apron. She worked. From the hour when the full-swing diggings were evacuated and the entire project quit in midstream to the day when they crept once more to the grizzled flat, as the dam seethed, settled and worked the body to the least disturbing depths, she stood alone in the cook tent and perspired. She fried her entire store of beans and hacked open cans of beef to last three days; she barred them from the tent and boiled coffee. They were sobered by her taking on and listened as she runted from the piece of iron on the ground before the stove to the plank tables, setting out tinware, blowing into the apron.

"It doesn't do much good to say he's buried in there," she heard Bohn talking softly in the sun outside and wiped her eyes, "why, it's just like saying, 'I've got a brother buried in the Rocky Mountains'."

Quickly she put the food in plain sight, untied the entrance flaps, slipped under the tent wall in the rear. With line, basket and rusty hook, she made her way to the tidewater and darkness under the one wooden bridge in the country, fixed her gear and sat down to fish for eels.

It was only one of many eyesores, one hump in a chain of knolls, adding nothing but an artificial lake, obscuring nothing but two hoof beaten points on opposite banks where cattle used to swim across and land. Whatever went into the making or whatever had fallen short of the great pile, it hardened in the sun, swelled at the base and now grew suddenly higher if watched in the pink light of noon. They were finishing it off. But despite the metal lampposts ready to light the crestway when switches were installed, despite the orange half-finished steel tower, bodies could still have slept full length in the crevices or been swimming blindly through the dark muck of the center. The wooden bridge downstream was gone, the cuts were dry, the old campfires gone out in Dynamite, old trails blown away and the sides of the dam left untraveled. Still, it drew spectators from the corn-land and at least one old woman back to its mountainous pathways, to accidental crags and ravines.

Ma fixed on her bonnet with mosquito netting and took up her basket. She left her skewing sticks and skimmer, wooden paddle spoon, file knives, tin cup and a heap of seasoned hot handle rags strewn across the stove and around the skillet. The netting with its black stocking patches was drawn over her head, all the way down her shirt front and tucked in the apron, two sides finally tied beneath her arms. She sat on the bunk with the covered basket beside her.

"There's other things of his I'd like to have," she said and pulled on a pair of shoes that had once belonged to the older brother. Ma, if she could have her way, or could get Luke to do it, would rob the barber shop of its museum, steal antiquities from the glass shelf in the window, hide his chary remnants from the passing eyes of strangers and men getting a shampoo. "There's things have feeling," she said, "and a use around the house."

His razor was spread open before the shaving mug on a square of Christmas paper, marked by a little card tied to it with yellow string. A nick had been cracked in the bone handle and there was scrollwork on the blade like that etched upon a naval sword. A bottle of tonic and septic pencil stood on either side. "There's more ways to skin a cat," the barber said, "than bury him," and for fifty cents the relics could be touched, a hooked shadow here, a bristling object on its back, gilt flowers of porcelain. On holiday nights he left a light in the window and on hot afternoons when the shop was empty he honed the razor, drawing it back and forth, achieving a Sunday morning shine. "No, sir," he would say, "those things are not for sale, not them." Smoothing white across the face or clipping halfway up the head of hair, he would add, "But there's postcards of them at Estrellita's."

Ma had all the photographs of his effects. It was the best she could do. She wrote on the backs of them:

"I remember this one, remember it well."

"Bought in Clare for twenty-five cents. I didn't take to the color. Right off."

"Cut 1 lb. fish fresh as it buys to four pieces. . . ."

The trails beyond the cabin called her, the scurrilous running of velvet pads was in her ears, there was a yapping in the air and the whole range to cover. She could go, the skillet was smoking properly.

"Now you put the idea out of your head. You ain't buying one of them concertinas. I couldn't stand it to be playing at me all the time." The Mandan put her short brown finger under the type and read along line by line until she reached the price.

The clamor of caged fowl drifted up, as seagulls used to cry before, over the dam.

Thegna loved Harry Bohn. She cut their letters into the bridge, as fishpole dangled and she slumped against the timber, and cut them into the yellow drying boards around her sink. Two boot trails appeared and gently sank in the mud; man and woman stooped together over hooks snagged in buried rushes. Behind them bubbled their heavy tracks. Hers were deeper. Never tucked in, hanging to the outside of rubber boots, her skirts fell heavily in the mud and dried stiffly in the sunshine when she climbed, Norwegian braids trembling against a sunburnt neck, to one of her sporting places. When the cook and man dragged across the river bed, if they paused, if he spoke or looked at her, she covered her face with red hands and shook, ploughing under little fingers of fish and churning the mud.

When his back was turned she freed herself and, cheeks blotched with the rash of laughter, swelled and cold, she stared at him through drawn eyes and rooted, as between fiords, toward the fishing ground. One had promised to marry Thegna, had married Ma instead, and then, in wedding suit and cut lip, hatless and with socks hanging below his ankles, had returned to honeymoon with the cook in Mistletoe. But he was faithless, black and cold. And she had never loved him as she now loved Bohn in the shadow of the dam and as long as it stood to hold back the changing waters.

She fried her catch behind abandoned pipes and gazed tenderly at the mountain, sticking thin bones into the sand one by one and slitting dead silver tissue with a jackknife blade. She cracked fire from stones. She wore her apron into the fields, through the destroyed paperboard houses of Dynamite. In her own day she had slept in every cabin now under water. No one knew how she came to be there —whose pure width stood welcomed among men, who wrestled heavily with the shade of laughter—but she shrieked when the first crew went to work, heaped broken sounds of affection on the black dam. She was clothed in sweaters from the warehouse, trampled among gangs, and beat a triangular gong of railroad track. As long as she lived, the wall would cleave back the earth, roads and river, allowing the bold to swarm across the bottom of the world and discover nests at night in abandoned town sites. As long as the mud dam needed tending, she would love Bohn, toolsheds and a dress dry-white with flour.

"I don't care to marry Mr. Bohn," she told the dormitory maids and no traveling justice of the peace tracked her, nor cursed her, nor made her cry—and carrying timbers one moment she could weep the next—no traveling teacher broke light upon her, no lover knocked her down nor left her, for he was dead. So she blushed at the least confusion and smacked her sides, as black shadows, wings and smoke yawned from every step she took and followed her. She smiled. She had not been away since the Great Slide.

Camper's wife took up her purse.

Coins, which at first she picked and counted behind shielding hands, laid one by one on the pile, mounted numberless and like lead across the table and quarters became dimes, nickels stone. But the disappointed women paused. They matched and bettered each card she turned with the same wry twistings of the jaw, they won by suffering and in silence; not clever, chinks missing from their spines, haltered by forebears and, large as they were, the prey of a few fork-tongued men, they won as they had been taught in sessions Biblical through hailing nights. They ate her money, it disappeared round the table and into the gullets of four usurers whose gold would never show, who hesitated to reach or even raise an arm before her face.

"That ain't my hand."

"You won it," Lou spilled the coins, shot them with the flat of her palm, "take it."

They sat as if still standing and their uneasy country gait knocked together legs ill-fitting under the table. Their thumbs were permanently scratched in ten years' testing for the sharpness of a blade and they had lost no blood. These four met on the seat of a wagon, survived Ma's wedding trip, thereafter packed away bonnets and allowed the barn to fall, fast friends.

Lou licked her diamonds. She moistened the ring finger first with the tip of a handkerchief touched to her lips, gently turned the band. Then she raised knuckles, bone, the thin stick to her mouth, gnawed as upon a hive, and one stone, another, ceased to roll and glittered in the center of the table.

With barely a whisper Thegna shut the door.

She had tacked no rawhide sheets across the windows, no smoke heavy on eyeshades filled the room. There were no watch chains on embroidered waistcoats, no weapons concealed in the finery, the feathered fronts of silken shirts. Black cigars, gold teeth, long wallets next to hot and scented breasts, these were buried under the young willow limbs of wing dams on the river.

"I ain't sat with a reckless player. Before now."

"Somebody give them to her."

"There's people wear such things."

And Thegna: "Don't touch them. Loan her, for awhile."

The cards were blank, warped as if they had been shuffled under water. The women held them at arm's length and to one side—to catch the light from a barn lantern shadowed by the faces of those with whom they boarded, shade lifted crankily to the lighting of a pipe.

"Don't you know Pa's game?" asked one.

"They play it even out to Clare."

"Let the lady study it," said the cook. "She don't know brag as well as you."

"I told him," pressing the cards face down against the table, "this place hasn't even a road to reach it. And, my God," leaning over them, "it's not Nevada!"

But the sternwheeler rocked upstream. Camper's wife heard the signal of the bells. The crystal glass palace, wide of beam, candles bursting in the darkness, plowed over snag and bar in the shadow of the dam. Smoke, and the music of an instrument strummed on the lower deck, filled the salon. From carboned chandeliers light fell on dirty cards and amidst the singing and dancing forward, the gentlemen, ordered not to wear boots to bed, with lace undone around their throats and black eyes flashing to the count of chips, created, among amateur and blackleg, a cold solemnity and harsh silence that would last the night. Wheels paddled sternward, only a few inches of night water separated the golden purse from the changing, uneven spine of the river bed.

"Sit down," said the cook, "he played!"

Again Lou Camper heard the ringing on the river, smelled tobacco and glass tumblers of brandy. They moved slowly at the speed of the lagging current, showering sparks on the black water, peopling with shadow and linen revelers an enormous liquid dead land far from shore. Feet splashed, shoulders scraped warm peeling wood and suddenly, from the deck below, against the constant lull of gamblers, a voice called up clearly between cupped hands, laughing through low fog and unaware of danger.

"Oh, Lou, Lou, where's he at now?"

ma was old already when she married the dead Lampson in the dam. And the Mandan was but a child.

She prepared herself in the morning, lasted and traveled the entire day to the wedding at dusk far south in Clare. In those days Ma had friends. They helped her, though they did not arrive until after sunrise. But, carrying her bundle out to the darkness, Ma filled her heart with the family rolled asleep behind, and knowing that wagonloads would find her, except for death or accident, thought not of friends but only of her tentative husband's mother.

"There's just one thing I got to ask. That is for Hattie Lampson to come. For her to watch it."

Ma put her clothes by the basin, filled it, and between the house wall and the roost, plunged thin tough arms and face into the water and after rinsing raised her eyes to twenty miles of dripping clouded sand across which lay the town where weddings were announced nearly once a month. She had heard of them. The pulse beat in the hollow of her elbow.

"It's too late for her," Luke's mother said the night before, "I won't go."

But Ma dashed herself with water and in the hour before dawn—she had lain awake to see a matronly night die down—she put a bounty on her own voice and expected, as if the very day could change her, to be persuasive in the ways of women. She shook out her hair. She soaked it. And the only thing she wanted she was sure of. The night before a wedding, perhaps then they spat and hard things were said against her; but on the very day of compliments, then the fires were set and the lock was on the door.

"She'll come around," thought Ma.

There were no holes from which wagons might appear, no hump to cross, no turning to bring them into sight. For miles of white land lay open and fallow on all sides of the ranch. But if they had to ride three days and nights and drive hard teams themselves, Ma would be surrounded by women married longer at her age than she could ever be. She patted her cheeks to draw up the color of the blood.

"I guess I can have my way. This once." Quickly Ma picked up the basin, flung it wide, and a shower of water splashed easily through the darkness.

In the open air, squatting in the sand for half an hour before the day of marriage, the woman sorted her clothes. She bit off a piece of thread. The gray hair dripped and slightly wet her shoulders. She tried not to listen for the stirring of the brothers and their old mother and now and then, wiping her mouth carefully, she raised her head and peered over the slight curve of the earth to the south where it would happen.

"If the sun don't come up soon," she thought, "I'll damp the pillow on our first night." And then: "I'll make Hattie Lampson dry it."

On all the days of the week, Ma never saw the sunrise though she awoke as early; for her the clearness of the day was noticed late and the first heat, which killed the very cry of the chickens, only wore her down by noon. But this morning she saw it gather, roll up and melt the east. The fire of the small, perfectly round sun was suddenly stretched, banded, across the entire horizon. She saw the thin red arms actually wrenched across the back of the earth.

"That's a bad light. But I don't care."

Luke found her hunched in a sun ray, head forward, hair laid flat on her knees.

"You ain't very energetic for a woman who's almost married." He picked up the basin. "You used the water."

"I'm entitled." Ma spread the strands. "But you ain't supposed to talk to me like this. You can't look at me, like he was out here watching what I do himself—before it's time."

"There'll be fuss enough," said Luke. "Just let me wash."

The head of hair grumbled. The cowboy took off his shirt.

"It's hard enough for me to keep my spirits collected without you around." Ma turned her back and drew the flowered satchel near.

"You aiming to carry something from the house?"

"I'm traveling, ain't I?"

"Right back to here. That's all." Luke blew into the water. "What's in it?"

"You don't watch me now! This finery ain't for men to see—except in the dark." She pulled wide the mouth of the bag and under spreading hair, arms deep, looked into the dust and flowers. For a moment, as the sun drew her scalp tight and turned the silver metal of her hair into powder, she slept and hands hung gently. Then, eyes closed, she straightened the layers and before tying shut the bag, stroked and settled whatever filled the bottom.

"People gave me these things. I'll keep it with me." On the other side of the wood and paper wall the old mother and her elder son were quiet. Ma listened for the splash of bare feet on the floor. The heat began to rack her shoulders and she heard only the scraping of the cowboy's fingers in the basin. He filled it again, trailing slowly down the sand and back.

"He's washing twice," thought Ma. She waited, thinking suddenly that she could have had it done in the cabin with the right man driven out from town and her own friends packed into the doorway. The sun brought it to mind, but the feeling passed as she thought of entering those streets that lead to church. She knew that in a moment she would want a long space to cover, a good many miles before sundown.

"Listen," the water dried on the cowboy's cheek, "you ain't aiming to take my mother to this wedding?"

"Yes, I've none to turn to."

Luke tilted the basin, poured, then stopped. He looked up—sky and desert shone tearless, clear, white—and rubbed his eyes. He dropped the bar of soap into the water and swept out the razor. He honed it once or twice against the sun, held it to a side of dry whisker, flourished and pulled. His young face had the acid smell of skin drawn under ingressive heat rays and his fist—it could pull a horse twice round on startled hoofs—was tightly fastened on the crook of the razor. After each stroke he held it outstretched vertically between his eyes. He aimed. The bright scroll on the blade that could twist the trickle of blood, turned white against his cheek.

Placing the razor on the wash box, careful to keep the steel edge free of the wood, he went into the cabin with shoulders hardly moving as he walked.

Before he came back, Ma saw the Indian child, too small to be a maiden, spying around the corner of the milk hut. The fingers of one hand spread stark and wild against the sod.

Ma colored, "You keep away from me today."

Luke returned with a towel. He rubbed on a fresh spot of soap. "No. She don't think she'll dress this morning." His mouth was hidden by a stiff arm. "I guess she better stay behind."

"I guess you shouldn't use his things! On a day like this."

Luke turned. He saw the hair which was fluffed out and starting to rise, the walnut ears, the fat shadow on the sand.

"He won't be shaving anymore. Not him."

Ma rose, laid aside the bag ready for loading, filled a bucket, and started for the coop.

"Don't wake him," she said. "Yet."

That was the day Ma sang. She carried a tune on dry nostrils and the Lampson ranch, by the sound of a woman's voice, livened in its bed of star thistle. Ma's song was louder when she passed the cabin, she raised it to leaning walls and the hidden flower of a man culled from the desert.

"My mother says it's time to start. If you're going to."

"I'll take her in my wagon. You tell her not to bother herself."

"She says she'll try to have a meal done when you get back."

"She can sit by me."

Three wagons rattled to the edge of the shell, as if they had been camped out of sight until the moment of noon, and slowly continued forward on salty flutes across the sand. Bravely three loads of women in gown and bonnet hymned together; Luke turned to locate the sound of women's voices, faint, from mouths already closed. He climbed on top of the sod milk hut and under brimmed hands watched the approach of old wives in the dust.

"I'm glad for you. They'll get here safely."

Ma smiled.

The desert filled with women. They swarmed within sideboards of beaten wagons, staring ahead for sign of well or a shade in which to dismount and shake. Three cartloads plied the desert. Banded warm members, they traveled free of the farmer and cattle driver, chopped to the roots stray outcroppings of slate colored grass. These were women who rode unwatched on the dry bottom of the lake with empty breasts and nameless horses, and even the oldest unsnapped heavy collars and soured the passing miles from the tail boards where they sat and dangled their weak legs. They nodded to the thrust, the side slapping of the wheels.

"But I believe there's trouble." Again Luke climbed to his sod post and waited. Narrowly he glanced at Ma. "Yes, sir. Them women don't have no water. Not a drop."

"That's all right." Ma passed quickly with the basket. "You don't draw such things to my attention."

"Well," Luke pulled on his hat, "I reckon they'd survive about anything." He walked away, sat down and watched her.

And those women were roughly able to sing songs of the skewered lamb and waters driven back by faith or oath. They were dry. The boards on which they sat, scraped of fodder, might have burst aflame if the sun were caught briefly in the eye of a watch glass. They traveled in three lifeless dories with dead oarlocks and rotted sails; they sang stiffly, managed to hold the reins. They backtracked, chewed the sand and made their way over weary, salty miles to see one woman their own age brought to bed.

Every one of them made the trip. There was not a woman in the desert who had not left the animal pens, truck garden patch and particular gully of the home to sit all day in the sun, to breathe the air of ancient lying in and love. For hours, under a never swaying skirt, a bare ankle remained chocked against brake iron or plank. The desert gave them up and they advanced; they might have died of thirst. But open-jawed and black, with matted and twisted cuts of hair, they crowded wagons taken from the farm.

They drew near, and Luke for the first time saw women's faces. Once again on the sod hut, a thin scout in the sunlight, a bent marker limp though standing, his own face worked, pursed and dripping as he watched. Bonnets, ribbons but no curls, skull-blackened and thirsty they stared back above the slick fronts of horses plodding low, stepping singly, flat and without wind away from wheels that were nearly locked. Instead of three wagon loads he would have liked to have seen just one face cleansed of the sun and that had not been formed and set long ago to the sudden bloody impression of a coffin bone. A few could not hear the meek but steady notes of their sisters' hymns and pushed their ears with hands that had been raised trembling three days and nights. "I want to see one," he searched among the tucked and tired wives, "before she's learned to keep shut. And outlive a man."

He did not wave.

"Smile," said Ma, "when you're welcoming." The sounds of iron pleased her. She would rise and accommodate them too when they actually arrived, not sooner. But once she paused, "Go get her," Ma hissed, "bring her here."

Higher than the sod hut or cabin, outnumbering the buildings of the ranch, they broke down in the Lampson yard. They drove across and settled on the ground where Luke had shaved. With spikes and nails working out of the wood, reared loosely above dead wheels, they hid the cabin from corral, cut off the roost. Only two front animals found room to emerge and hang toward the south and open plains on the other side. All those women and a dozen horses mauled in the first enclosure they had found since setting forth. Luke climbed and stepped among them. Little spars, a few carrying flimsy woven heads of sage, balanced with the slack, tipped and dug into the ground. The air was filled, below voices and slowly slobbering bits, with the steady descending sounds of rope and shroud, skirt and ringlet.

Ma, too late, suddenly cried out: "Don't get down!" Carrying the satchel with both hands, smiling, snapping her eyes, she darted from wagon to wagon. "Keep your seats!"

Luke hid among the horses; he unbuckled them. Bits slipped in and all the way out of crooked mouths, away from square, flat, slanted teeth. Breast collars were hung loose and low and the weight of wagons dragged against forelegs instead of chests. Tight cruppers wrenched the raw high ends of tails, bristling and gray, pink and choked, straight above the mounded rumps and to one side.

"They must have last had this gear on cows."

A few big ears were pinned back against manes under headbands that had ridden up, and as they stood like burned men dumbly waiting for cindered clothes to fall away, the harness slipped aside from cuts and abrasions. Steam rags had been ironed to their sides and stripped off. Large hoofs, one before the other as if to step, were planted—unpared blocks of chalk—on loose ends of leather that had dragged the miles of the journey. Blister beetles sat on the brass terrets or suddenly still, fell dryly to the ground.

"Ma," he caught her arm while she continued to hasten, to urge and push them up again, "we can't reach Clare today."

"You load this bag. And fetch me Hattie Lampson."

"Don't listen," answered a small, steadily nodding voice, "don't pay none of this family heed."

They swept back, made room and left Luke Lampson's mother her own bright place to stand. She waited, then spoke no louder:

"You're all welcome." She nodded, this little woman darkly turned out of the house, this last and oldest divulged by the desert. "I'll see you off." She looked at her younger son, but took no step. Ma caught her arm.

"Hattie," Ma moved her, "can you get up on that seat alone?"

They stood her by the wheel. They stepped back and the old woman shortly swayed, a stalk snapped upwards from the sand by the iron, mud colored rim, a length of wire coiled and motionless in the spokes. The great pinwheel might have ground her cleanly into the dust and she would have crawled away with skin unbruised, with dry pulmonary parts intact. She and the wheel—its tapered bars, sanded rays, were longer than her two arms fully spread—looked as if they would never move again; one, the original means of carrying them from Boonville to the bloody plow handle, the other, that which was originally carried and turned to love in the night's wagon ring around the fire. But had it turned, and had she fallen, her kerchief caught in the spokes nearest the ground, she would have hung before her feet once more touched the settling, noisy track. And when the wheel did turn, smoke hung thinly about its tin bucket nave where wood burned against wood and miles wound in carbon around the axle.

"You ride in the one behind mine. Mulge comes last."

The animals awoke. Amid the scraping of slowly prodded hoofs, the slight sway of warty food buckets and rope ends under the wooden bodies, Ma remained at the front of the train holding his mother.

"Put Hattie right up there. That's it, by me."

Luke in the second wagon and his brother in the third did not join the singing. The horses, as large as they were, crouched down to pull, their legs spraddled outwards like the flappers of young and panting dogs. Each wagon carried not only its own sounds of travel, the tug, twist and strain of the wooden windlass, but was loaded with the clatter of the other two and moved—one wagon could never make such noise—across the plains like a house athwart rollers.

High on the first prow, wedding bag under the backless seat and the sun softening the wool of her dress, Ma leaned in front of Hattie Lampson and spoke to the driver. The ranch, with no men left behind and guarded only by the Indian child, had disappeared down its faraway indentation in the glazed sand.

"Swing us a little to the other way. I sense it more to the right."

The woman sawed the reins.

Thus they traveled a dog's pace on an enormous field that once, perhaps, had been cultivated with shrub, tree and herb, now extinct, which swelled before their eyes at moments with a few head of cattle, with larvae that clustered and disappeared. Not another rider or wagon train crossed their path.

Ma held her hand clasped to her eyes and peered through the thin red line between her fingers. She sat high, a gunman who had crossed the route for forty years on a rocking coach.

"A mighty lot of you turned up."

"Yep," said the driver.

"Hattie," Ma spoke louder, "I'm much obliged. Since you changed your mind."

The mother of the Lampson boys said nothing, seated in the open heat between a woman almost married to her own son and another still married after rearing five grown men. For Hattie Lampson was taken during the trip to town. Her flat, boneless nose was cold. She nodded.

86

"Clare by dark," said Ma to the driver, "maybe sooner." She shifted. Her long skirts pulled, and she changed her chin to the other hand.

Hattie Lampson began to mumble on top of the hymn singing and turn of the wheels.

"I'm indebted to you ever," said Ma and put her arm around the dwarfed shoulders. "You been here to give me courage." Ma rattled, looked at her quickly and gave the cold little woman a rigorous and sudden hug. She snapped free. Ma eased her again under a brown arm and widely ruffled sleeve.

"Hattie. You ain't going to be doggish. Not on a wedding day."

They rode unmolested over the flat pan—fifty miles away there might have been a mountain range to seal them perfectly within the white disk passable and clear—and looking way to the ground Ma watched the last of the hoofs, so slowly dropped, switch and explode in dust. She felt under the seat for her finery.

"He's probably thinking just like me. Now," said Ma and fanned herself.

Hattie Lampson spoke: "He wasn't brung up for such. Not to be handed straight over. Naked. He'll work some now. There ain't no family. There ain't even any boys, men neither. You can't pass them all out. They're supposed to laze around home. Take care of their own farmyard, they was told.

"They get no pardon. It ain't just any hound can go out shorn and keep his head up. I say they're done. My younger has gone just like him. Bringing that Indian into the house is about as bad. Neither one can hold himself straight. They was behind my back.

"Around their age they start feeling worms inside and nothing I say will change it. Why, he's been walking you sideways for two years steady. And when he won't touch no food, there's enough to kill him right there.

"Some just worm themselves in. I ain't going to be touched now the way you do. You ain't going to get me to help you mix no water in his meal. Just to lie spread in the dish. I got to watch for him and keep him quiet. But I'm not sure he'll make much noise anyway. Folks forget. They'll forget the whole family.

"They won't even remember what month it was. And he won't, for sure. No one knows mine neither. You ain't going to live long enough with my boy to get the yellow off his teeth or bleach out what I learned him. You're too old.

"It wasn't much. About when to come inside or out, is all. And if he's found presumption to do more—and be offensive to some for the time being—I guess you ain't going to get any good of it. Least to your face.

"I ain't a person to have stood up for either one of them. I don't like to see a man worrying about whether his hat is on to front or back. And taken to traveling around on foot, tucking at his shirt and leaning down to loose his shoes. But as of now I cut them off, the two of them.

"Maybe a woman ain't fit to make something of them in the first place. Maybe I done wrong. And mine is even worse than most. Wherever them worms come from, that's part the trouble.

"If you can be like me, and I ain't ready to admit that, your trouble might not be more than mine. But a bad dog just gets worse. I ain't sure what you'll do to him; I won't thank you for it."

"Hattie," Ma dropped her arm, "you better draw breath."

The begrimed driver shook the reins, wiped her face and looked at the old woman. "Mrs. Lampson, you shouldn't question so. It

ain't right for you to hold out so harsh. This girl's pure as snow."
She drove again.

"Hattie just ain't feeling well," said Ma. "We got to overlook it.
She come along for the sake of Mulge and me. That's enough. And
she's going to stand right up there in front of all them people whether
she's sick or not. So we got to make allowance. She'll be nicer when
it's done. Won't you, Hattie?"

For the last time his mother spoke and stopped mumbling. "I
don't know anything about snow. I ain't ever seen none."

They rode without wagon headed sails. Lava and a few skull
halves cracked beneath the wheels. Towards dusk a wind from the
surface of the sun swept their path and blew against them live,
lightly running bunches of gray wire and weed which sang against
the sides of the wagons, across the burning bush, caught in the
spokes and harness, stuck like burrs in the horses' manes. The storm
passed, hardly ruffling the discomfort of so many old and rigid
women.

Clare was nothing but a spot on the plain where the sand thinly
billowed, kicked up by someone crossing the street, stirred by the
closing of a swinging door. The women sat straight and smoothed
themselves when they saw the small constant geyser raised by the
mere presence of a few men. The horses suddenly began to pull, as
if they too, heads to the ground, could see the camp town—Mistletoe
was less than that at the time—and the hitching rail near the bare
wood church.

They were stopped by a shout from the Sheriff.

"You can't bring all them people in here. No, sir, not without a
license!"

Luke, not his brother, climbed down. He beat his hat against a sore unlimbered leg. He tucked in his shirt, loosening the muscles of his arms and back, drawing up his chest, and walked the length of the wagon train to the Sheriff.

"Howdy." The man in khaki pants, knee high boots and Stetson, never left the barroom porch.

"I don't see how you can keep us out," said Luke.

The Sheriff leaned back against the post and again put the knife blade to his fingernails.

"All's I got to do is call my boys. Of course, if you scatter, it'll take us a little longer to round you up. But I wouldn't." The Sheriff brushed the parings from his vest, leaned forward and pushed the blade down a patent leather boot top to scratch his calf. The uncut nails on his red hands were longer than the manicured.

"But this here is a wedding!"

"Don't matter. I don't care if the whole pack aims to rut. You the man?"

"No, sir. I ain't the one. That's sure."

The Sheriff raised his head and slowly scanned the wagons, looked at the quiet and waiting eyes of the women who stared back. In a low voice he muttered to the boy who stepped closer and listened with his back to the train. Then louder: "But that don't make much difference. This town's got a law. My men would be here in fifteen minutes, if I called."

Luke heard the knocking of the horses. He smelled molasses and rubber gum, gun grease and a handful of browned leaves loose in a hot pants pocket. And suddenly he jumped onto the porch, two short steps loud on the swaydown boards.

"Well, now!" The Sheriff squinted.

Luke whispered in his ear. He spoke softly, using all his breath, against wax and smile, his own forehead near thick temples, his boy's chin low to the bulging collar. He broke out as he felt the air fall from his throat, not caring that he was unable to see the other's eyes. The pistol butt pressed upwards against his thin stomach. The head bent slightly forward, looking for a damp match dropped in the dust. Luke spoke into it with haste, perhaps asking how many cartridges the gun would hold. The ear was yellow since the squat man, in jest when drunk, bragged and fixed into it the moist end of a smoking cigarette. Luke shut his eyes.

"All right," the Sheriff gently stopped him, "let them by."

The Clare geyser churned and climbed suddenly higher as they rolled.

Ma married, by bonfire light and to the music of a borrowed and portable celesta, in a roped-off lot behind the church which, at the last moment, she refused to enter. At some time, after food was found, and away from the crowd of women, Luke spread out his neckerchief and said to the Sheriff, "This here pie's for Maverick. She ain't never seen a wedding."

Throughout the night, Luke's first in town, and until the middle of the morning when the trip home was attempted, Ma sat alone by the stretched, flat, feverish body of her husband's mother. Ma's chair faced the open window—it was a short jump from the strange and empty room to the ground—and at her feet lay the satchel, tightly closed, and the old woman who cried out, in the racking of her shoulders and occasional thump of her hand against the floor, for sleep. Ma sat straight and listened for the sound of returning footsteps. Now and then she leaned down to dry the darkening forehead or touch the plaited hair already wild.

"You did come. And I've married me a torment. I deserve to sit here on a folding chair, not even able to ease you off to sleep. I nagged you the whole day. And all's I got is a bare finger which, had a ring been set on it—and you was right to keep it back—would have been yours, since he had none to give. It wasn't mine to take. Nor was he. I guess it ain't just me he's shown he's got no feeling for. And I can't make it up to you. Since he's left us both."

rounding the corner of the Buckhouse—first four-sided, wooden shanty built among the tents, first building to turn a red false front and open hinged door on the dry grass and shapeless hills—Luke Lampson slowed his walk and stopped among the travelers still outside.

The Buckhouse had almost been a town itself and the prows and ribs of longboats, brought in by flatcar and having never reached the river, stuck up on either side in place of rock, horn, plant or door-step in the sand. The tide had passed, leaving a small anchor and a few links of chain in the Buckhouse acreage which was marked at the farthest point by an old keg in a drift, blown over with weeds. Railroad tracks had come this way and gone. Now the slashed screens and narrow door, the green booths and back room out of town limits, faced on the highway and remained in darkness despite the head-lights flashing up and past. But the frame house shook with the rumble of tires.

"What are you fellows doing here?" Luke Lampson untied his

tobacco bag and squinted into the changing colored lights that flickered outdoors from above the bar.

"Leaning, Luke."

"Just leaning."

"Watching the people driving by."

They squatted in the grass by the red wall or stood, shoulders hunched against the planking, staring off at the night sky or up and down the black road. Their carrying sticks lay across their knees, ends fastened to personal belongings bundled like cabbage heads at each man's side. Or the sticks were propped in a row at the wall, like racked rifles, and at each man's toe there rested a woven football filled with undershirts, shoelaces and packages of glazed saltines. The red neckerchiefs, freshly tied, were new. Their coveralls were heavily dusted from the land they had crossed and they talked together, rustling newspapers in the darkness, of the last automobile they had seen.

"Been many on the road?" Slowly Luke fanned his hat. Heads leaned farther back, ears were scratched, possessions laid hold of, bugs flicked to the grass again. And one of them mumbled:

"About three hours back there was one. Four door."

"Two door."

"I reckon it was four!"

A magazine, with a zebra-skinned woman on the cover and pages damp—retrieved from a hole in the foundations of a barn—was held up to the light and admired. From beneath one pair of coveralls there thrust two shiny leather boots. A leather jacket could be seen at the collar and from the breast pocket there hung the broad white elastic strap of a pair of goggles. He did not speak but watched the cowboy with the rest.

"That must've been the car I met. Parked up the road apiece where the driver's kid was snakebit."

They stirred as if to rise and settled again, the spy among them silent, faces turned to the shadow.

"I reckon not. I don't reckon a car like that'd ever stop out here."

One pulled a bright new harmonica from his pocket and began to play. The man with the magazine finally turned past the cover, and from across the highway, where the store had competed with the Buckhouse ten years before, there was a sudden rustling in the brush and a pebble dropped into a hidden well.

"Keep a good watch, boys," said Luke and squaring his hat stepped inside and up to the plywood bar. He was watched as he entered and the wheeze of the mouth organ softly faded.

Those who might have remembered that ears had been chewed off long ago in Buckhouse brawls and that women from over many borders, slipped by lax patrols, had been forced to whirl their skirts hip-high at gun point, had passed to other diggings and other cabarets of dried earth. Only a few, remembering how the fights and women had pushed their way outside and over to the porch of the store, driving the keeper through his rear window, lingered close to the old places, within a range of twenty miles.

The spangled, tinkling lantern shade, with red beads and panes of blue, still slid and turned around the single light globe, filling the quiet, summer evening air with twitching, faded streamers of color. There were twenty-two caliber bullet holes in the ceiling.

"Bowl of chowder and shot of muscatel," said Luke. He rested his foot lightly on the lead pipe rail and stared, pinching his chin in his hands, at the cans of beer pyramided before the dusty mirror behind the bar.

"Bohn been around tonight?"

Revolving slowly, the tasseled lampshade turned the men first red, then blue, and caused dots of color to walk across the brown photograph of the dam over the mirror. The trestle, with small, erect figures holding tools posed stiffly at arm's length, wrinkled, even under glass, across the wall. Ma had always claimed to be in the picture.

"Hey, Snake-Killer!"

Luke turned and in the last green booth, blurred and heavy in the colored lights, shirt unbuttoned and pulled aslant from white chest, he saw Camper laugh, flex the fishing pole in fat hands.

"Cowboy!" He stooped heavily to draw a match sharply on the dance floor. "You didn't expect to see me again, eh? Or the wife either, I expect. Well, she ain't here!" With both hands he caught the edge of the bench and laughed, turning pink as a new chip of glass slipped into place. Red mosquitoes clung to the shade.

"Howdy," said Luke, and whispering, "I'll take my drink and chowder at the table."

Luke grinned, pushed his hat back over one ear, and the two men shook hands strongly, the cowboy's arm rock hard at the elbow. Camper, with three empty glasses and fishing gear neatly spread before him, flushed, and suffering the bites of insects, still deftly and without a tremble held a reel to the light and probed, tuned, with the metallic point of a miniature screwdriver.

"I couldn't keep away from it," he said, "even if she hasn't got much water in her. I had to see it."

"I wouldn't go on her in the dark if I was you." Luke watched the eyes; they stared between white ears battened to the skull. "There'll be more water in it than you think in the morning."

"Just so there's a foot to cover that lousy yellow ground, I don't care. Couldn't wait for morning. I know that dam like I know my own golf course, every hole and trap in it." He rubbed at the mosquito bites and for a moment was quiet, looking at the browned newspaper shot of the project above the bar.

"No. By sunup my wife'll have the kid dressed in his swim trunks for traveling, the radio tuned up, the car loaded and headed towards sandstone and the line. I wouldn't catch a thing."

"You aim to try her in the dark?"

"There's no wind, is there? There's no danger, is there? They surface at night. I'm a hunter." Camper twisted the head of a pin in the reel. "You took me for a tourist!" He reached across the table and shook Luke by the shoulder. "A sightseer! Why, hell, I was crawling around that river bed a whole year before they got anything like a staff of men out here. And I watched that boy drop out of sight almost before my eyes. Here, take a drink of this."

They touched glasses and threw back their heads. The harmonica played again beyond the door.

"Say, listen," said Camper, "before we get talking about it, and I know he's your brother, I got something I'd like to ask you."

Luke nodded, tightening his lips.

"I want to make a trade."

"Well, now," Luke lit up afresh and grinned, "I never mind a little bargaining." He had bargained for Ma's stove in a vacant barn on the edge of Clare, won against twenty bidders. When he bought his fourth plow pony from the Indians and paid them by note, the Mandan came with it carrying the tack, because of the color of his shirt and ferret jaws.

"I'll oblige you. As best I'm able." Hearing a slight sound or sensing that slit eyes had opened, darkly over his shoulder he added, "You keep yourself out of this, Sam. And bring another bottle." His own eyes were on the man stopping in town just for the night, who might make off before sunrise, leave quickly when there were others on the street or be two hundred miles away before finding himself the loser. Luke never moved his head.

"Well, I'll tell you right off." Camper leaned forward and flatly said, "I've got to have those steerhorn boots of yours." He drank unsteadily and spoke before he finished wiping his mouth, "Got to. They've been on my mind ever since you fixed up the kid."

Luke slumped back against the soft new paint of the booth. "I never do anything without considering it." He spoke softly. "What would Bohn think if I gave away my boots?"

"But I'm talking about a trade . . ."

"How could I drive the team?"

"You don't need them like I do . . ."

"Besides," Luke tucked his feet back under the bench, "Mulge give me these boots. For my birthday. We drove clear to Daisy—that was beyond Clare and over the line—to pick them out."

"But look here!" Quickly Camper reached under the table, fumbled, and pulled up a yellow sandal. "I mean to trade!" He gave it to Luke.

And after a moment: "That's different." Luke held it forth to the dim colored lights meant for the skirt-high dance. "It sure is."

"Go ahead. Try it on."

The cowboy studied first one sandal then the other, felt the white rope soles and yellow leather thongs that crisscrossed the foot from toe to ankle. Weighing a soft piece of beachwear in either hand he called again over his shoulder, "Don't you worry about me, Sam."

"Here," whispered Lou's husband, "just let me feel one of those steerhorns . . ."

"Leave that boot alone. I ain't done looking."

"All right. But I played golf in those sandals. I wore them at the best beaches on the coast. Took them right in the water too. I loaned them for a night to the prettiest woman I ever saw . . ."

"I never do anything easy."

"I've driven over the whole country with nothing else along but those very sandals. Why, I even took them into the army with me . . ."

Camper pulled, squeezed and tucked the cuffs of his flannel trousers into the carved black tops of the boots, touched the shiny steerheads on the leather, scraped off a bit of dried earth under the arch and stood up once to feel his weight slide back on the wobbling, worn down heels.

"These sandals ain't too uncomfortable," said Luke.

The torchlights of the welders were another steel ring higher on the turbine tower. Ready for coffee, the night crew looked away from the glare and saw, through darkened hoods and across forty miles of clear water, the sharp handsaw ridges of a country from which the air had been exhausted.

"I used to come across all kinds of things every work day." Camper sat with his legs crossed to the side of the table, nodding one boot up and down. "Dishpans, wagon wheels, anything you can think of. Why, one afternoon I even found an outboard motor. I cleaned the mud off, scrubbed it, worked on it, nearly got it going too. But you was never down to that river bed often."

"I kept away from it pretty much."

"I know. You was on the range when it happened. I heard later. Well, I'll tell you, I never got over it."

The watchman in the power house, wearing new striped pants and a trainman's cap, dozed in a cane bottom chair tilted back against the steel plate of a moistened wall. Current was passed from contact to copper contact in the machinery pit, and the seismograph took down the track of the earth and progress of a blindly swimming man inside, in erratic, automatic writing.

"I only knew him by name." Camper kept his eyes half shut and talked as if to a widow. "I'm not sure that I ever really saw him at all."

"I never seen him much myself." Luke's eyes smarted from the wine.

"But I knew who he was—after," the other said quickly. "I remember when we were in the payroll line. I'd hear his name called out somewhere way up front. Then he'd yell back 'ho!' and I always knew that fellow was early for the right occasion. If there was new equipment, he'd get it, no chit or nothing. If there was a free medical inspection, he'd be there."

"He wasn't good for much around the house . . ."

"Well, I don't know what we'd done without him, working the way I hear he did."

"And as far as going into a field or on the prairie, not him."

"But he went on the project, right down into the trough where a damn big river used to run, worked with machinery that could chew a man to pieces." Camper kept his eyes on his hands and drew one of his long matchsticks under the nails. "I can tell what it must feel like, having a brother like him. I know you got an idea of what we all went through.

"I saw him," Camper raised his head and forced down the other's eyes, "only I didn't know it was him. The engine was moving out to the end of the track, over our heads of course, the mud was sticking around us tight as ever, we sang a little, just about time to quit—and it happened. I looked up, shovel lifted about to my knees, and saw three men on the top of the new section. Two moved a little dirt, I could see their straw hats nodding around, boots turning in the mud, slowing down, waiting for the whistle. But the third one, standing further up where everyone could see him, why, he'd already stopped. There he was, just leaning on his shovel, just propped up there not even bothering to talk . . ."

Luke jumped from the booth, sandals cracking flatly on the floor, and ran to the bar, holding it with one hand, pointing at the project photograph with the other, "See him up there? That's my brother! Mulge, what do you say, Mulge?"

The black car pulled sharply from the highway, drove straight at the Buckhouse and parked, hood flush against the door, headlights filling the room.

"Lampson, what are you yelling about?" wheezed Harry Bohn.

"I'm Camper," said the fisherman as he introduced himself.

"I shouldn't have let him out," said Camper's wife.

"But all of us had a hand on him," laughed a squatting welder.

"Why didn't you stop him, then?"

"Slipped away," said the welder.

One boy, one Mexican, and the white haired linesman who had flown slowly from north to south in bird ways and built transit barracks on the plains, lifted their eyes to a woman's golden quarters and felt, smiling or silent, their white ribs. They had sucked the saguaro in the desert and bred fungus in the bottom of their shoes. They pulled each other's teeth with strands of unraveled hemp. Their helmets lay upturned at their sides in wait for another softening of the earth or for news of waters gathering again at the head of the river into which, years before, they had waded stripped to the waist and ears still loud with the clattering of Thegna's iron.

"It's too late now. But," stooping low to another face, a woman searching the hordes on litters, "where would he go first?"

"Not far, lady, but none of us dared follow him too close."

"You," quickly to the next, "where would he go?"

A few sat with hands folded on shirts spread across their laps, covering their loins with leaves, one polished a small fruit against his thigh. A towel, fringed like a Spanish shawl, draped a pair of shoulders, one head was capped with a handkerchief knotted at the corners.

And sullenly from down the line: "Maybe he'd hunt up Luke."

"What's that?" She looked for the man who spoke, hurried from one end of the white shot wall to the other, walked more slowly now to choose between three or four. All shook their heads, none moved, men slashed by cable, once felled in the tracks of the donkey engine.

"Maybe not. Might call for the old woman."

And ten men down: "Anyway, you wouldn't catch him in to Clare."

"But, lady," Lou Camper saw, pounced on, the moving of the lips, felt the brass end of his finger rub her slacks, "we don't dwell on his coming back." And the firm finger touched her again.

"They'd riot again if he come back."

"That's right, after all we mourned."

And from the drawling boy: "Not every town would make as much of him as us."

"We'll leave in the morning then," said Lou. The men nodded. "Who," smiling at the boy, "would know him if they saw him?"

"Everybody. But," raising a half cured cheek and open mouth, "he'd be a sorry sight if he showed up." The Mexican, neck of the guitar resting against the hollow of his hip, reached into the bucket, drew forth a foot nipped by fish, dyed purple on the brown. He pulled it into the light.

"You," said Camper's wife, "do you remember him?"

For answer his head bowed over the gravel.

"He'd be forty years old now," a brisk voice started, "and not liked near so well."

"Lady, don't ask us any more."

Before men who paused long in the quarters of the moon and hid possessions quietly in their rolled shirts, she thought of the small dog returned to the forgotten bush and the small town scratching for its son.

"In those days you could have followed him down the street."

"That's right," a moment later, "in any place but Clare."

The night was loaded distantly with the smell of old shell cases and powder already shot. The welders, unlike hog men or men of the hills, were unable to keep silent in front of her, their mouths were not stunned shut and awry. And now and then, to break the stare of the silken woman, they mentioned him, a brief description of wet wash as telltale as his small footprints in the mud, the sound of their voices through larynx and nose still pinched and awed with the knell of the one death. There was no flood but of light, and in the light no clash of cocks or bodies, only the lime glass garden and woman whose whispering relations with any one of the sitting men could have sacked as little and exposed as much as the accident which, with a clap of land, had rocked the little purgatory.

"And if he stopped, you could have touched him."

"If you caught his eye, and if he'd heard your name."

Old Lifeline lay in the darkness before her men, no longer muddy but pocketed thin as rainwater over the pits of sludge. The tidal, raft-bearing sweep of her was gone, her gray capped current locked in a few poison berries dried by the banks. Her pitch evaporated, the flood pulled from her like the tubes of a butchered ox; she licked without stench or stomach the lower crude pyramids of the dam, above it, barely covered the rooftops of impounded farms. In the days before, howled upon, steeped in froth, she had rocked the speck of a cowman seated cross-legged upon his bobbing horse, had matted many a dappled mane and washed afield dog-paddling ponies.

But now, from Mistletoe to the end, to her most remote and dismal channels, and to the sea, she lay, with gaps from bend to bend, bell clear above the burdening offal. The welders were sometimes called upon to point her out. They had to kneel low to dip their hands at noon.

The young boy dug at his heel and a shiftless rattling of the pails sounded instead of lap of water behind the dormitory. None of them moved and, each to his stool, sat in file as if one hidden hand of each was wedged, trousers covering the manacles, into a split and gripping rail.

"It was hard to believe he was gone."

"Turned his back on us."

"Some of us called him, hollared after him from the bluff, damn fools that we were."

"There was one soft sound that would have raised your hair—like a great animal digesting bran. Him or the dam we couldn't tell."

"Jonah."

And after a pause: "Except if it had been a whale, he might have escaped."

At that moment one Red Devil, lost from the rest, dashed to the edge of light, stopped and revved his engine. Standing with legs spread eagle, holding the machine quickly in both hands, he nervously twisted the throttle grip, blasted the sand with exhaust, and looked over his shoulder toward the trailing dogs. He sat like a bird still flying, in dead motion the wind still seemed to flatten his driving clothes. The small and wary goggles flashed in the floodlamps. The starting pedal vibrated beneath his calf. It was loosely wired to the oily makeshift frame. Now and then a short claw tugged at the strap around the neck, the knees bent rapidly up and down as if the heels were about to shoot in all directions and he twitched, pulled at the chipped and battered motorcycle and lifted his nose toward the freshly scented path. Behind him the scampering dogs with rough fur and winded ribs, jaws clamped on hanging tongues in the over-country race, drew near with forced cries and shaggy heads, bewildered in the sudden opportunity to run. With each crafty burst of the engine, the barks, a sound hoarse and long unheard, started anew. They seemed to be running through the air, these animals lured from under stoops and from the foot of tumbled dusty beds.

Suddenly, small oblong head jerked toward the men and woman cowered at the wall, he raised his fist. For a moment it jutted sharply from the sharkskin body. Then he crouched, kicked his feet, and sped diagonally across the lot like a thin and spotted deer before the bough stands of fumbling hunters.

In the following silence they stirred again, one coughed.

"You see, mamm," whispering, still watching the hole in the darkness where the rider had disappeared, "we ain't forgot."

Lou Camper climbed slowly to her feet. The dogs did not appear.

four men stood at the roadside. They were led by one who seemed to know the country and who, as they paused, scanned it with the scarred and suspicious eyes of an old strong man. They had left the Buckhouse quickly but still were far from the waters behind the dam. Only now, out of breath and brought to a rustling stop by the pain in the largest's legs, did they begin to talk and touch shoulder to shoulder, bumping in the darkness.

"How are you, Bohn?"

"I'm ahead of you, Lampson," pulling the fat but beardless chin, "because you boys don't have to try so hard."

"Camper," interrupted the perspiring fisherman, "remember that name?"

"He heard you," murmured Luke.

"I knew his brother," persisted Camper to the old buck, nodding at Luke, "by sight, anyway."

Harry Bohn bit the tobacco plug, three inches long, round as a broom handle, then swung himself away and faced the north. The hair on the sides and back of his head was a tinted silver, black at the ends in the darkness.

"Harry, he can't think of anything else, is all," said Luke.

"I can't either," said the Finn, twisting and hopping, "and I'm going to get back to town, Bohn, where I can do something about it."

"You stand right there. With me."

In the broad and gray cat face the quick eyes shut and opened, and Bohn's small lips, thin and stunted from a touch of the wailing forceps, yawned over a little cavity and trembled. "We'll go on together, both of us." He lowered his head, clenched one hand into a fist, grunted, and with the other gently rubbed his burning heart. "He ain't open to the public," feeling his trousers with the calmness of age as he spoke, back still turned to Camper, "no matter how much they crane. Get as old as me and you know that."

Harry Bohn, by miracle born of a dead mother and thereafter in his youth—he looked quickly over his shoulder lest he be caught thinking of it—drawn to the expressionless genitals of animals as the Sheriff was in a later day, doted upon the stomach kept distended with effort, and lest they be torn to pieces, slept with his hands drawn in from the edges of the bed. "You're lucky," the doctor told the boy before he fled, "you wasn't buried with her right then and there. Now be good." And in the darkness of the night, with muscle of the athlete pitted against the hermit's birthmark, he briefly stepped aside for the passing of water—as another might turn his head to cough—and swallowed a black and spongy pill picked from a matchbox. Then Bohn burst with feebleness and fought, with laughter and pains of senility, a past in which life moved deep within the woman's body though her hands were cold.

"I'm still ahold of myself, Lampson. At least I ain't out looking around like these boys here."

108

"We're just walking, Harry."

"I know," attempting to make his bass voice crack, "looking around for sweet tooth."

"We're out to fish," said Camper and tapped the dismantled rod.

"I got shirts to wash, lighting wires to put across the floor, Bohn, with half my fence down, a window lead to hang and plenty of time except you use it all!"

"Finn, you ain't nearly home yet."

Except for Bohn each might have run his way, ducked his head to escape the dark and empty road, the still plain from which, even at night, the buffalo could be seen to creep. All but Camper, who might have wandered to his death. The spare men—they had hands that were of one piece and put to purpose like the head of a hammer, bodies that appeared to have come first through the mist of nettles, skin which over a period of time ejected splinters, were obviously men by the hanging of hat brims and the constant sound of their breathing —shook the dust from their clothes and rubbed their shins as if they had stumbled on the way. Camper urged them forward, the Finn back. As they talked, picking at each other's sleeves, they looked up, listened for the faint jumping of the fish or cry of the wolf. It was not only Camper who, unto himself, licked his mouth for a taste of the imaginary spawn of game and feared through the night the foot-fall of the hunted. The great natural wilds lay around them without dens or lairs.

"I got to go back, Bohn. I got to rope my cabin down. My place isn't going to be swept away!"

"What do you worry for," said Luke, "when Harry's with you? My mother worried about the same thing. She said it after Mulge fell in the dam. But One Hundred Acres Grassland ain't going to turn to dust."

Camper quietly stepped back and waited.

"All right. Shake them canes on out of here. If you want to."

Luke no longer heard them. The fisherman, the cripple, and the old pink-cheeked man were bent aside by the wideness of the sky and in a moment, with hard lines at the corners of his mouth and crowfeet white at the points of his eyes, he returned to the image of his mother and heard her chair rocking on the gravel. Rarely he thought of her, but if so, if it came upon him as he plowed across the dam, he checked his horses and held them to a standstill until she passed. He saw her now, sitting uncovered in the sun a few yards from the cabin. She talked to strangers, pointed with crackling fingers toward the fowl she could hardly see. Even after the Slide and word of the death that brought her own, her voice would suddenly begin beyond the silent house. "That one there that lays," he heard her, smiling at someone come to mourn, "I like her, and the one next by it I had since a child, and the one that's blind and chokes when it crows, and that one with the comb who can't crow, I like him too. And that other, that's the last, she's a good bird." He could hear the visitor take off his hat. His mother scraped her rocking chair in the sand. And it was at such moments that, receiving a passerby, she talked as a young girl and coyly rolled her eyes. But, by a trick of age, the pupils disappeared and only the whites remained in the posed head above the smile.

"Look," said Camper, "fish won't bite after four o'clock."

"What good will they do you?" The Finn danced on the metal beneath his heels. "You'd better be out taking pictures—you got a flash?—or buying some mosquito dope if you aim to stay."

"Harry," Luke shook himself and touched the black-winged arm, "shall we show them a thing or two?"

Slowly they started up the road.

Properly, absorbed in care, they prepared to bury Luke Lampson's mother on the bluff. The body, not changed the least five hours after death, strong as ever in constitution, had spent no time in the Lampson cabin but waited for interment helplessly by the side of the grave. That morning she had predicted hail. Luke spoke for them all: "We better cart her over before it starts."

But a calm settled on them when the spot was reached, firm sight of the trench fixed narrowly in the ground determining each to take his time. They made allowance for the storm. Deliberate movements and dry throats, long faces and speculation lengthened the afternoon and suspended the effects of sun and cloud. Her last word done—Luke sent a message with the body—no argument was given in the presence of his mother and not a memory nor bitter sentiment invoked. Each suggestion, and members of the party wished to express no more, was wrapped in several minutes' contemplation and answered in silence by those immediate to the dead.

Hattie Lampson wanted to cause no trouble. After her prediction, coming at the time it did and despite the morning sun, was taken as more than a warning and caused Luke to walk far in the empty lots for horses, she forced quiet even upon herself and attempted to appear asleep. But the eye of a woman who felled eagles with a rifle and downed them to bounce in the dust with heads smashed by a single dum-dum bullet, fluttered and refused to flatten permanently until she spoke:

"Don't leave me about this house. Just put me over Mulge, just lie me so as I can look down on him."

Her surviving son's old friends, receiving the actual remains among them and charged with picking the location, repeated the message to each other several times until they straightened her on the ground they thought she meant and dug beside her. They sighted along shovels and determined that she hover where she wished.

"Do you think she might find it better down aways?"

"She can't be fooled. There's just one proper view of him. She knowed that, even when she ain't been up this way for months."

They nodded and neatly tamped the sides of the grave. The distance between the words that came from her own mouth and the choice they finally made, by disturbing the earth, was great. But once at work, cutting a thin cube and shoveling a place that would be ringed round with visitors ever after—since she was specifically located and he was not and few wanted to traipse a whole mile and perhaps not even find him—they felt her satisfied and spoke no more about it. They were the artisans, even less concerned with her long life than the lawfully compassioned who gathered as quickly as they could and stayed until the burial, when ended, brought a hasty darkness following on the edge of the storm.

She died young. Deformities around the mouth and unraveling lines in face and hands were hardly honored by those who peered some hundred miles to the sunset and who said: "She looks to be about the same, I guess." Except for the Slide, hers was the first Gov City death and, catastrophe or not, was the first natural death among them. Many were as old as she in frame and flesh, were just as keen and liable to the same youthful, pretended sleep. But they were allowed to attend her death and stared long, now and then, at the sleeveless gown and shoes hooked on her at the end.

Hattie Lampson had not been snatched away. Man or woman, perhaps they expected the sudden disappearance, the fault in the shell of earth and death between shifts. They had clamored once, found nothing to do, hardly anything to see. Wreaths, if available, could never be dropped from a safe spot into mud. Cries and an excuse for history came by accident without an hour of sorrow or memorable handling of the dead.

The completion of the grave was the first event, accomplished more rapidly than planned with the easy removal of the lumps of earth. Arrivals appeared slowly. Climbing the bluff, they paused for breath and, having been told where they would find her, face up and sleeping as fixedly as stone—there was no chance to lose her—they looked heavenward and speculated on the cloudburst. Without alarm, more reticent than ever, had they decided on or even wished for the construction of a coffin, it might have taken forty days to ready, working on weekends and in the evening. As it was, the earth was excavated, tools already cleaned and out of sight, and nothing remained but to take their time and study her, discuss it, seal her in and loosen on their heads the hail that waited in abeyance.

Perhaps a slight wind should have hummed across the miles of black land, bearing the faint lowing of faraway cattle or the sound of wheels grinding on Luke's wagon. But there was only air enough for each and no sign of her living son until he actually carried her hand-chest into their midst, seesawing heavily on his shoulder. Ma and the Mandan stayed behind him.

"Sit down, Luke. There's no rush."

They pointed to his mother on the ground. They used no nails. Hers was a fair embroidery and the expression on the closed, depressed face—wise at the small curves of the mouth, a few scattered inclinations on the brow—was the same that settled on or pinched her when her boys had not come home.

Luke sent her out of the cabin to the tableland when she died. He sent her into the charge of friends who, while he cleared her things, expressed to herself, not him, their sanction and willingness to help. He left open the door and windows when he set out with the chest and the two women who, including himself, Hattie Lampson in the end firmly claimed to be her family.

Not many wanted anything from the trunk. Her last deposit, it was divided into one pile they could choose from and one to discard. She herself had once pulled the travois that carried it. Now it was lightened and, as hinges noiselessly crumpled, was relieved of the furniture of the dead. They took without asking and gave no thanks to a process that bestowed upon them only cloth and clay.

Each man present looked at her, not having to breathe the heat, loosely covered, and some noticed that she no longer wore her spectacles and that the lids appeared white and tired: "But not her face in general, mind you. Don't reckon that's changed at all."

And each man recognized to speak with a friend or two and, if silent, looked long at strangers as if they also had touched her and taken up some trinket from a dusty pocket, an object slowly appropriated from the crocheted shroud. A few left empty handed. But, while on the bluff, jaws set and without moving a pace, they stalked in the sand the pleated, stitched ninety pounds of the dead.

Her son, who never had listened to her, lay below. She was on top, shaded by followers, clasped in a small rigorous attitude beside a grave that did not gape nor call attention to itself. Those mutterings that were not speech, but which she unconditionally declaimed and seemed to have meaning to herself, were done. The peppered, flat sealed nose, the small sloping top of the skull wherein once lay the secret of preserving health in the dry heat of the afternoon and of remaining lazy, this aboriginal shape of hers was done with chores and elevated to extreme old age. Not having died in some drinkless caravan blown under the sand, not even strong enough for a trip to her son's grave mile in final days of life, it could at least be said that she would remain intact as long as any in earth or burial cave. They readied beads to drop beside her. The volunteer, who undertook to fulfill her own last wish and make of her a landmark, to dispose of her, to make and break a final contact between the live and dead, squinted toward the plain, then at the halted sky, and shook his head. He lifted her.

Face down, eyes in the dirt, she peered through the sandy side toward her son below, where he too lay, more awkward than she, feet up and head in the center of the earth.

Graupel fell thickly from the dark cloud. Freak pellets rained on them. Drawn in a group to the edge of the bluff in the direction which she had pointed, they saw nothing of dam, hills or river bed. But they heard through the sudden storm the clank of machinery and the shifting voices of banks of men, the sounds of chain and engine and at times the thick coughing of boots in the mud.

Old and widowed, Ma picked up her divining rod from its hiding place.

She had walked far and now was tired. Knowing as well as she did the dried wagon tracks, the empty contours of the land that slipped into darkness, it had still taken hours to cross at her slow pace the silent fields and cracked grill slabs of earth. She stole through the box cabins, the small reservation of Mistletoe and heard nothing of the card game or the welder picking his guitar. She reached the edge of the bluff.

Her divining rod was hidden near Hattie Lampson's grave. She shuffled, leaned forward, spread picked over foliage and scratched for it. She was inclined to sit down and rest, to catch her breath, slip the bandage properly over her sore again, to ruminate on his mother's grave. Ma's day was long—she knew how far away the horizon—and she could not sleep. For all the hours and all that could be said about the one woman whose death she had seen and knew first hand, there was no time for the smaller grave. Ma had not thought highly of her.

She picked up the forked branches of the rod. A sigh issued from sorrowful lips and cracked with the sparks that ruffled the dragging skirt and apron. She stepped from the bluff to the dam, crossed the town line to her husband's grave and the stick twitched, jerking her in sudden palsy across clods of sacred ground. She hung to the twin arms of the branch, and suddenly, on the crest of the dam between lake and plain, looking backward into a darkness that bespoke no city, she called:

"Oh, Mulge. Where are you, Mulge?"

And she cried no more. She searched across a few acres of the mountain—cliffless, rounded, without danger—as though planting spiked leaf or weathering flowers before a reasonable headstone. She sanctified an immane body of land and depended on the divining rod. Old herself, distracted, now and then her mind snapped back to his mother who visibly had spoken, tottered, folded wings and died. On one side swelled the artificial sea over cabin, gulch, and bedstead, washing against the dam and nests of barometric instruments hidden in cut rocks by the engineers. Below her the rows of boxed fowl stretched from dry bank to bank and the birds, now crying and fighting in the night, dropped feathers through chicken wire and filled the river bed with a crowded, sleepless scuffling.

Ma turned to the voice of the dead. It sounded once against the bottom of her feet and trailed out of range. Slipping from the peak of the unfinished road, she dropped from sight, descended to the shadows of the southward slope and, driving the branch into open furrows, labored after it with concentration she herself might spend in dying. Ma stopped, pulled garments tight, squinted and hurried on. She lifted herself to the persistent tugging, the call of the husband dead by accident, and upgrade and down she circled the shadow of his remains. She knew, she understood these signs of the young shoots crushed in the darkness, the sudden appearance and whirl of insects.

Had he jaundiced and died, lay sickening in the cabin in open shirt and socks hanging over his shoes, he might have pulled Ma with him, down with grief to the grave, or she might have grown immune as death revealed him. But now, spared the slackening of strings and nurse watch through the night, having lost him without doubt midway in the growth of a mountain, she firmly sought to find the slow and unbreathing, blackly preserved, whole and substantial being of the dead man.

She spoke of him infrequently. But the squeaks, rustling of feelers and roots in the night stilled her ladle in the iron pot and made her glance with suspicion at the warm sleepers. She came to him on foot.

Her clothes pulled loose again and she stopped. The shafts of wood leaned against her and the invisible team, which drew her onward to unseal the earth, slackened in night harness. She worried, heard bits of falling clay approach and fade, she shook the white train of mules into a quick gait.

"Mulge? Hold in there, Mulge," and the divining rod plowed at his heels. Ma opened up the grave—each widow has her mile of road, the dark ridge of her adopted name—and she revealed signs of her striking loss in the furls of the earth. The whole town had roused at his death, but it was Ma, drawing closer to an unmarked entrance through the years, tuning herself to cries that were still in the air, who grew thin, brittle, until of hardly any flesh at all, only an obligatory grief, her age and heavy shoes weighted her to the ever settling soil. And Ma, more than the others, actively pined away and opened many graves to find one full.

In the night and on the dam, Mistletoe's dead man was hers, one who could walk but not breathe, who, without recollection and face obscured, still whistled as he had before when Ma cooked and Luke was never allowed to stretch out on his brother's bunk. Ma drew near. But the steps, the dragging shovel, everything that pained and pleased her, retreated and slipped further into the darkness.

"Luke ain't been no comfort. He ain't given me one kind word and no provision. Oh, Mulge, I can't go on this way."

Ma's was not a replenished vessel but an iron pot, not oil but scavenged vegetables, and the creditor had come leaving her few words thrown out, downcast lines in the face, the short, forlorn speech of the lonely woman. Hands figuratively outstretched after death—now clutched thinly to her person and which, thrust into the coals, did not burn—these she crossed on her breast and at night while standing up, these scratched against the cloth of her shirt for comfort. She struck at the air, received only impaired sensations from the long gone and heat rising from awkward waves of earth. She drove at her interminable circling, picking bitterly and with thin strength at the gates of the tomb. The white mules of the widow sway easily round her secret mile, ears straight forward to the sounds ahead.

Even now she heard the silence of the crowd as it stopped and the earth closed. And for all those who had watched, Ma only shook her head; for those who had moaned once, she shut her eyes. She never spoke to Thegna. In the rumor of friend and enemy she was robbed, before death and after, so she staved off other women and worked apart from men. Her eye was weathered in the wildness of the dam, her mouth in pain—open to the hard air—when she called him.

Ten years of death and the year of married life were shaken loose, dissipated in the gyrations of the divining rod. Dead leaves unfurled at the tip. She tramped in the field scaled to hold back the waters; she walked on dry seeds that were picked up and blown by the lightest warm wind and, left to the family in the cabin but hardened against it, Ma raked steadily a ground of iron, scratched the spine of the desert. But she could not touch him, could not lay hands on the black sleeve.

Ma had made that clothing, or at least fastened it together with thick welts of thread, allowing no rips or tears to be forgotten, embossing them in painfully raised stars across lapel and knee, arm and elbow. She clothed him as she fixed herself, in black summer or winter, buttons bound so no claw, fist or wire could pull them loose, pocket flaps and cuffs, hem and frill removed, saved, fastened at last across the frayed place of wear or fresh hole. Death took every stitch, clothes fell from her back. And stumbling where Luke drove the horses, smoked, and plowed, Ma saw the jacket of the dead—blacker than the earth itself—that made her breathing hard and caused white animals to veer noiselessly and pick up their trot.

"I deserve him back like this," she said. But he was gone. The dead whistle in summer through fixed teeth, stones are gently raised on riverless cracked banks, and in the mildness of the small town, roped in from the desert, spectators, with boots on teetering rails, stare up and down empty, flickering streets. Whole families wander the surrounding country, hands in pockets, kicking sticks of shale and overturning rare bits of wood.

Ma perspired in the darkness. Ahead she saw Luke's lister drill, squat, unhitched, tilted against the slope of the dam, seeds mildewing in its coffin box, burned out and black like a piece of armor on a battle hillside. Drawn to equipment, to a wagon loose in a field, to the numberless, lopsided wheelknives of a harrow abandoned by the trickling stream, she touched the rusting metal.

Ma climbed to the worn crosstree—bolt and chain clinked beneath her—and holding to the locked brake handle settled herself to rest on the driver's seat. Her feet dangled, heels thudded against the hollow wood. She leaned forward, chin in scarred hands, and breathed faintly the odor of horses long since unharnessed from the burden. Miles from the Lampson place, seated quietly in the middle of acres which only Luke dared tread upon in daylight, Ma moaned and nodded as if she had lost him only the day before.

"I've let him pass me by tonight."

But, eyes staring at the flat of her apron, face buried in stiff fingers, she could not hear the quiet footfall, the close deliberate opening of the earth, the parting of the weeds.

She could not see behind her.

On impulse, throwing off his coat, Cap Leech, in the days when he could shave a cow's heart thin as glass and determine with one look beneath the sheets the life span of the stricken, dared to extract the secret of a dead woman; on a wintry morning, having arrived according to law too late, he attended the birth of Harry Bohn. The mother, dead but a moment, gave up the still live child in an operation which, hurried and unexpected, was more abortive than life saving and, when the doctor drew back, lapsed into her first faintly rigorous position. The son, fished none too soon from the dark hollow, swayed coldly to and fro between his fingers. Leech left his scalpel stuck midway down the unbleeding thigh, buried the wailing forceps in his shiny bag, stepped outdoors with the infant and disappeared, thereafter, through all his career, barred from the most fruitful of emergencies.

But attendance at the surrounded bedside was not his special pleasure, he was not keen to treat night after night the umbilical cord like a burnt cork. He did not care for the sight of a swelling that decreased and felt no duty to bring relief to a woman lying in a shaft of sunlight. Her only discoloration was for a purpose, and Cap Leech believed in the non-usefulness of burst organs; no good could come of it.

In the days following his clandestine operation upon the corpse, days of smooth cheeks and high collar, he teetered between the whiteness of a hall and the spotted robe tied behind the sufferer's back. His training had begun with a set of wired bones in a dry box—he had clicked the teeth—and ended with poppy leaves smoldering in a pharmaceutical brass dish. Unguentine on the tip of his finger, reference to the tight page of a textbook, a limb swaddled in lay wrappings of bandage, the count of clear blood cells like constellations; with spectacles and shaved temples he took to searching coal bins for the wounded.

Cap Leech was no more a midwife. A family of one son and one unborn had been abandoned for earaches and faeces smuggled in milk bottles when he set out with a few sticks and powders for thirty years practice among those without chance of recovery, doomed, he felt, to submit. With him went the child whose features he had touched off by a slight grazing of the tongs.

He wandered the fields and lifted, dropped arms. At times, appearing starved and old, he answered questions and advised upon the description of a sore or at sight of a smoking specimen. He cauterized, poked, and painted those abrasions and distempers which, when healed, were forgotten or which, at their worst and sure to enlarge, brought a final shrinking to nameless lips.

The box grew brown with age. Once, in the empty frenzy of a cold night, he flung the bones across a whitened plain. But, always in time, he discovered the marble counter, the revolving fan, and jugs of pills. He crawled jerkily across the gumwood floor, stethoscope pressed upon the shell of a beetle sweeping hurriedly its wire legs. He mixed a foamy soda draught in paper cups, dust in water.

An old obstetrical wizard who now brought forth no young, losing year after year the small lock-jawed instruments of his kit, chalking black prescriptions on the leaves of a calendar, he was reduced to making the little circuits of malignant junctions, in conversation only now and then with a crafty druggist. His skills became an obsessive pastime and he looked even at the hobbling animal with a heavy eye. Warts appeared on the medicine man's hands.

"He's in there."

"We'll run him out."

"With the Sheriff. The two of them."

The wagon was burning brightly. Red light danced on the wheel tops, curled from beneath it and flitted up and down the steps which appeared to be driven into the serrated earth. The onlookers, Wade at the head of them, watched, spoke in gentler tones before the untied horse and leprous, flaking chimney.

"He's got a girl with him," one accused from behind. They stirred uncomfortably, huddled at the caving rear of the jail.

"If he has, he'll make known of it. But none's been brought this way as yet."

Wade shook his head, in a whisper promised, "Better than that. He's a man with knives. Wait and see."

They could hear the muffled windy sound of a choked voice, the righteous tune of one who continued to talk even when closeted with the Missouri madman. "Old Sheriff ain't going to be stabbed," grinned Wade from side to side. More soft now came the Sheriff's muddled sermon through drifting leaves, as something, a dream, slowly stopped his mouth.

"You, Wade, you been in there?"

"Ain't anybody going to put Wade in that wagon, are they, Wade? Maybe he couldn't take care of himself like the Sheriff."

The horse sniffed the milling of the men. The head waved, hard of sight, feeling in the darkness for the hand with a rope. He was roman nosed, carried at the tip of his skull a broad sloping pad of fuzz and moleskin that had been cuffed when he refused to ford a river or rise in the morning to the traces. He was one that would stand when gimp-legged farmers came out to ask for help. The slack pockets in the nose closed in winter; in summer he snorted, the long ears lay flat. The tail switched, swept between the shaggy legs, rolled briskly into the black pear rump of an animal a fraction blooded with the mule. He turned his head away. From the desert other signs—a missing sheep, a carcass—now awakened the linings of his nerves. One foot moved, returned.

"When's the show come on? When's this fellow going to bring out that girl?"

"Or a two head calf."

"Or a baby in a mason jar."

The door opened an inch, a crack of fire, and was sloughed shut again by a helping shoulder. It opened, swung to, was pushed like a shutter from the nest of flames, and Cap Leech, careful not to smash his hands, stepping backwards, lifted the drowsy Sheriff into sight. They stood on the narrow platform of the top step from which Cap Leech, who now held the Sheriff's faintly reeling body with one thin straight arm, had squinted at an early and voiceless dawn, scratching his face. With the other hand he picked at the lawkeeper's hidden shirt front and the tip of a long white sheet was tossed back into the fire.

The Sheriff continued to swing his head, mumbled through mis-

124

fit jaws, "The Range and Prairie Almanac never lies, the Moon don't stand still. You bide by what I tell you." Leech propped the Sheriff, took quick small steps to make of himself a ramrod. "If you don't listen," said the Sheriff, "I'll fall." Odors of disinfecting floor wash and spirits of ammonia drifted from the red door.

"Boys," Wade tried to free his arms, "they're dancing!"

Leech had heard enough about the almighty moon, pituitary of the wheat field and cow in foal; down one step he went and, catching the Sheriff around his waist, set him on the ground. He was light, round with talking gas. Cap Leech pushed back the head and folded the numb fingers in the pinched cup of the lap. He turned and for a few moments walked a circle some way apart, hands in long pockets, pausing now and then to stare for twenty miles through the darkness where rose one discolored furrow, a rib of earth that wormed for half an inch above the rest, as if it had been plowed up and left to dry, a spot on the horizon, the dam. Out there not a living creature, no wrist to count or old flank needing salve—he had lain his touch on animals also, in a stockyard razed by fire, had peeled the white fat glue from under bellies or driven his knife through an open eye to the brain—and he returned to the doped figure of the Sheriff. He rocked back and forth on his heels.

The Sheriff looked up, tenderly felt his temples, tried to speak, and stomach doubling in noiseless spasms at the same time, swayed as if someone boxed the sides of his head. "Quackery," he said, awakening, "quackery," and searched for the bars of the jail. His mouth was full of aspirin and the taste of steel.

Cap Leech unpocketed one slender hand, drew out the squeaking tongs carried in his trousers like a small key, and pushed the Sheriff down again to the step. He aimed and held the fat man with the ball point of the instrument, gently tapped the softened breastbone. The Sheriff wriggled at the end of it, ogled upward with drugged eyes.

"Now," said Cap Leech, "I'll talk."

"Wade there will clear my head."

"What you been doing to the Sheriff?"

As the law officer tried his legs and wobbled in the dark fernless yard behind the jail and Wade bounced after him, Cap Leech climbed to the top of the splintered steps, sat quietly and watched them. His mouth cracked a line to see the Sheriff sternly sway, nearly topple, an aged guinea hen with shattered cerebellum and aimless walk.

"What did you do with his revolver?"

Leech, the goat who sat in the hunched position of a man, shrugged, stroked the two long forks of hair at the end of his chin. He picked the back of his hand blotched with the corrosive action of cheap chemicals. He watched the Sheriff feel himself with wet fingers while the moon-faced friend, calling in a hurt voice now and then, attempted to learn what he had tampered with. It was a warm night and Cap Leech had cut again as he wished into a foreign town, a soft head. Sight of the Sheriff still on his feet gave him as much pleasure as those whom long before he had left helpless on a bed of white.

Wade and the Sheriff rolled from the shadow on stiff, rubber tires, a topheavy tin pickup truck. They swung it silently in a half circle on the edge of the light from the nearby wagon, stepped back and admired it. The Sheriff, suddenly stooped to spit forth a long dark string, motioned Wade to attend the truck and tottering, amazed at the slime, felt a bird body hot from his intestines lodge in his throat.

A bunched comforter covered the front of the truck—the frail engine, the flapping fenders, the hole of the radiator—and dragged on the ground. Wade tore it off, a matador sweep of dirty cotton. He began to crank but the narrow engine, so worn and without gaskets, still made no sound, turned over with no resistance, loosely. It was a truck that carried both man and animal, rear floorboards chopped from the toes of pigs, a truck to be seen at night with a woman's knees down to the running boards and in winter left frozen in a field.

Cap Leech's horse poked his overhanging nose toward the truck, sucked his tail tighter and returned to gazing at the plains. Cap Leech whistled softly through his teeth to see if it would start.

There was a cow in the back of the truck. The sheer and luminous udder swayed lightly through the slatted planks and, as Wade cranked, the red calf gently bounced, tossing the velvet ball. It was a youthful cream head of cheese, a nodding pendant, and the teats protruded only faintly, the knobs of new horns. The Sheriff walked slowly to the side of the truck, reached through and stroked it. The little hoof stamped, the immature red color, pink and brown, quivered in his hand. A smell of new milk and oil, manure, and brake drum fluid filled the yard. Between the red wagon and the truck and backed against the last adobe wall of the jail lay the fresh row of motorcycles, already entwined with corn stalks, webs of dust. Flies and sac-tailed insects moved in columns across the broken spokes. An accumulated late night buzzing came from the heap of confiscated machines, a warm and smoldering pile of metallic fodder.

"Is she gassed up, Wade?"

With weak step, still sick, the Sheriff returned from the jail weapons chest and carried under his arm the hunting shotguns.

Sighing, clutching the truck door, he stacked them, blue bored canes, behind the feather and sawdust seat. He climbed in and wiped a clear spot on the windshield.

"You better come with us in the truck here," called the Sheriff.

"I'll follow," answered Cap Leech, "you can't drive faster than the wagon."

Wade brought the cannisters of shotgun shells, sank behind the wheel. And Cap Leech flew in his wagon, pointed the horse in chase, running neither in trot nor canter after the red back light of the truck which, without splashboard and no vehicle to lust, sped toward Mistletoe.

He kept no hold on the mad horse but gripped the edge of the springing seat, spoke to the deviled ears now and then, a rootless spectator to the burning of the twenty miles. The horse, having never flattened himself along this course before, was guided by the Sheriff's lamp; Cap Leech, having stumbled upon the rotting stones and stories of his family grave, rode willing to take one look, no more. The deodorizer of the homestead watched for the first sign of blackened wood and a narrow door cut with an air hole of a quarter moon. Ahead he saw the young cow hold her bush up uselessly for love or rain.

As if they had been lying on their stomachs in the flat sand, four muffled men jumped from the side of the road, ran hobbling and with yells to wait toward the slowing truck, climbed on, pulled up the last, and crowded the cat backed calf against the planks. The men clung to the red neck.

"Ain't room for us and her too," Harry Bohn boomed into the wind, "I better come up front!"

"Stay where you are," answered the Sheriff. Seven skirted Mistletoe, raced for the lake.

In the wagon Cap Leech trailed behind the suspicious travelers, hearing their wordless clutter in the darkness. He had the power to put them all to sleep, to look at their women if he wished, to mark their children. Tie strings streaming, eyelids fluttering in the wind, he pulled from his vest pocket a roll of powdered lifesavers, began to chew.

In the truck Luke tied the whipping hat cords under his chin. Camper cowed before the patched white head of the calf and the near naked Finn hung his stiff legs over the speeding track. Chicken grit was caked on the accelerator.

In the wagon a lone occupant rode the bow of fire and with a tarnished frozen thermometer pinned to his breast brought something of clear vision and bitter pills to the fields of broken axles. A tin can fell backward and landed at his horse's front hoofs, sprigs of straw whirled out of the air ahead to stick crookedly in his ears. They threw a dirty glove in his path.

In the truck Harry Bohn caught Camper around the ribs. For the first time that night he allowed the fisherman to stare at his humming-bird lipless mouth. "You," he shouted, "untie that rope!"

In the wagon Cap Leech watched its body float down upon him, larger and larger. Horizontal, feet out straight, Pegasus of a branded species, he expected to catch it flattening in his lap. The calf lay on her side in the air, about to crash, pink spots spun on the red hide and a gentle whistling loomed over the wagon. She disappeared. Then Leech looked down and there on her back in the road she sprawled with milk rolled jaws, albino eyes in wrinkled pads, and a clean crack splitting the amorphous skull that struck; nothing more ugly than the placid mask—its mouth roared wide enough to eat meat—of a shocked cow twisting upwards in the moonlight.

And in the truck, "Sheriff," Bohn knelt at the windowless hole in the back of the cab, "I'll owe you for your cow."

"Don't stop," the Sheriff kept Wade's hand from the brake, "we'll catch her on the trip home. If those devils don't come upon her first."

✝ he last time Luke Lamp-
son fished the bottleneck his brim hung down with rain and, amidst
lonely flotage, he had felt the water dragging at his feet. It was a
rain of sickness that drove the rest away, that filled the bottoms of
a few cattle lofts with alcohol. A rotted poncho wrapped the sentry
who, for an hour, was left alone in the floating countryside. The
beady cigarette smoldered in the damp mouth, and his eyes looked to
the right and left at the grass rising above water, at the sunken clouds.
He would never again be dry. Some vast spider lay on its back with a
shellful of warm fluid, sleeping through the rain of an afternoon.
A pool began to whirl, then disappeared; distance had never been
so great nor so flatly ruinous as when the twigs rolled by on the lagging current. He moved only once to shake the water from his hands.
Otherwise he merely listened, watching the end of the bamboo pole.
A small frog rose from a ripple, blinked its head, clung for a moment
to his boot. His wide misshapen brim dripped in a steady circle.
Across the western body of water not a fire burned.

The white line tugged the bending pole and he began to draw it in, a long cord from the whale's belly. He felt no pleasure as he squinted to find the hook breaking that low water run beyond its course, only a drenched habitual motion waiting for the surface of stripped branches. Minnows beat more slowly in the basket over his shoulder. The slant of the line reached his feet, the end of it still carried under by the catch, dragging, slow to rise. He lifted the huckleberry pole and there, biting the hook, swung the heavy body of a baby that had been dropped, searched for, and lost in the flood. The eyes slept on either side of the fish line and a point of the barb protruded near the nose stopped with silt. It turned slowly around and around on the end of the wet string that cut in half its forehead. It had been tumbled under exposed roots and with creatures too dumb to swim, long days through the swell, neither sunk nor floating. The white stomach hung full with all it had swallowed.

God's naked child lay under Luke's fingers on the spread poncho, as on his knees and up to his thighs in the river, he loosed the hook, forcing his hand to touch the half-made face. His hook cracked through the membrane of the palate; he touched cold scales on the neck. One of the newborn sucked inside a gentle wave to the bottom of a stunted water black tree, its body rolled on the slippery poncho while the crouching figure of a young man shut his eyes, wet his lips.

In both hands he picked it up, circling the softened chest inside of which lay the formless lungs, and stooped again to the water. As his feet moved it thickly eddied, splashed. He held the body closer to the surface, water touched the back of his knuckles, and letting go, he gently pushed it off as if it would turn over and quickly swim away to the center of the bankless stream.

Luke again huddled into the poncho, casting a pinched eye across the grayness of the flood.

The water lay above the roof tops. It stretched thinly for many miles away from the great missing forks country.

"Wade, stay in the car," and without another word, they kicked through the silent sands in a broken, faceless line to the water's edge. Not a gull circled their heads, there were no rushes from which the crane could jump and fly with its ill-concealed legs and gawky call. The last drippings of the river lay eighteen feet deep, currentless and pure as rain water, backed without roe or salamander into the shallows. They stood on the low banks like men come upon the severed cathead of a ship or the small prints of wandering herds. All but one stooped to search for his own footfall. In the darkness, a few dunes broke surface, still wet, lean as rocks which before had been merely slopes in a rolling earth.

But even when trying to stand still in the face of the watery discus and stare, if for only a moment, without comment or restless sound, the sands gave way under their feet and they fell to an erect wrestling, laughed suddenly at a hat kicked a few yards along the shore until it landed crown down and out of reach in the water. There was no bean can or grappling pine—the shotguns lay in the truck—but still enough darkness and promise of a wild sunrise to excite them to paw and stumble, a few to expose rashly their seedy chests.

"We all got wounds," beating the Finn to his knees, "all of us got a share of dickie bird heads desquamated on the river banks," and the overbearing shadows purled at the moist edge of a hundred and forty miles of milky water. The last of the brooding wranglers laughed for the first time that night and Bohn, now out of their way or batting in their midst and at the cowboy's side, felt something graze the soft mealy sock of his trouser front.

"Go on, tell about him," nudging with a familiar elbow, "go

on," said Bohn and began to cough so that both the top and bottom lip of the small mouth—sometimes he dreamed that he could yawn—paled and trembled more thin than ever, pursed by the bitter doctor's fingers. Luke thought of that slim and vertical mouth as carrying a hook, barbs lodged in the roof years before.

"He was a big baby but a little man. Ma said Hattie told her." And when they laughed: "She used to keep him covered out of shame for his size." The rat toothed Lampson, last of the brothers, spilled to them an image of a load too big to move, described, with shoulder sucked into Bohn's armpit, a man too frail to be crushed. " 'I'm in love with a fence post,' Ma said before he went."

"His first mistake was just sitting there."

"He isn't going to hear. . ."

"Well then," above the scuffling, "he's not so mighty. In the house or out he was the same, like he was petting something inside his shirt."

"He didn't love animals, I could see that."

"He didn't love anything if he didn't build, not an ark or bridge or landing. All I need is a sandbag and some warning. . ."

"You ain't going to be buried, Finn, you hear? You're going to drown. That ain't a warning either."

"But Ma tells how Hattie used to speak of holding him, used to rock him behind the house. She could hardly talk, trying to show her head around the baby propped against her shoulder. He stared back across the prairie all day long."

Once out of earshot of women, they baited the ghost. Only a quarter mile west of Mistletoe with its kerosene shades and dotted pokes, the six men suddenly became true to the whips inside their arms, shook the fat on weathered legs. Had they a jug they would have drunk then sloshed playfully, horses prancing after water. The sand slid from under their feet and to the bottom of the lake; and to that corner of the grassland field there fell now a knee, now a hand. Their clothes rustled with the sound of dry rattles stuck by insect mucilage to the bare skin of their calfs.

Bohn took off his vest covered with ashes, then his shirt. "Come on," he said, looking at all of them, wiping his weak chest and flexing a tattooed tombstone on a strong arm. But the Finn jiggled out of his way.

The laughter stopped.

"Who's he?"

"You don't hear everything all the time, Mr. Bohn."

"He never crossed my town before."

"Come over to Clare more often," said the Sheriff, "and you ain't going to be in the dark so much."

"Bugle belly," said Bohn, "I don't want to see you."

Luke Lampson stepped apart, close to the man who, short as himself, had interrupted without a sound. Moonlight hit the stranger. He stood poorly in the sand with flashing spectacles, bare head. It was a waning moon, brilliant for a moment on the same warts, the same long lips and the little scowl shrunk from the sun. Luke could see, having never before touched bone of his own, the stains of contagion that spotted the face and hands like shadow, representing the white worlds through which he had passed. And in his pride, filled with the traveling surgeon's shriveled broadcloth and his shiny temple, Luke looked quickly into the butternut eye and down.

"Pa," he said.

They walked to the water's edge.

The small boat was like the hollowed body of a bird. Its keel was a breastbone hung over with dry calking, waving splinters, one not sunk under the mud when the great forks disappeared.

"Keep out of that boat!" Bohn fastened his dirty cuffs and peered at the hull as if it lay snapping in the sand. Luke picked up the iron stove top that was its anchor and dropped it in the bow. In the darkness he pried the bending oars from under the seats.

"The fact is," catching Luke by the arm, "you're just going to stay on dry land."

Luke pushed gently and it slid from the firm beach into the water, continued its downward slope ready, with one more foot, to swamp, then righted itself and sat low in the moonlight.

"Get in," said Luke.

Camper had no chance to settle in the stern but, hunched and muttering, began immediately and with short bruised strokes to bail, to keep himself afloat.

"I promised him," Luke said to Bohn. He held the floundering rowboat by its limp rope.

"Cast it off," whispering, "let him go plumb to the bottom."

"I'll call Wade," the Sheriff tried to lean between the old man and the cowboy, "it'll cost you fifteen dollars for a personal fine."

"Sheriff," with a quick glance, "you ain't spoke well of my brother tonight. You ain't got no say in the matter."

Ten years before, the skiff had been dragged and carried overland, pulled by running men from where it was stuck and abandoned in the river gone dry, upwards on the slippery south face of the dam and faster down the northern slope. They had struggled with it a few hundred yards into the basin, panted, wiped their foreheads, climbed in, and waited for the water. The boat finally rose with the lake. For two days, until a shivering in the current brought them again to shore, the men, who had forgotten to provide oars and who had no sail, waved to the crowds gathered to witness the covering of ranch houses and the land.

136

Camper scraped its insides with a tin can. In its best days on the river the chubby boat had been splattered with fish oil and moored at night to a barnacle covered pile; now it loosed its seams and sank slowly under Camper's hand.

"Pa sits in the bow," said Luke.

"It won't float the three of you." Bohn turned away and darkly chewed, refused to look at it.

"What's that you got there?" asked the Sheriff.

"It's what we use to hold the oars. I'll row."

"Oars!" Bohn spat into the white sand. Then: "I'll tell you, Lampson, we'll send the Finn out in it, you stay with us."

The white cane shot through the air, landed point down like a small harpoon. The Finn swung his bolstered legs to retrieve it. He snatched it up and propped himself belligerently some distance off. Then, seeing the signal of the oars drop with finality into place, he hobbled slowly back toward Bohn.

"You," Cap Leech suddenly spoke as they slipped away, "you've come to no good."

The Sheriff, Harry Bohn, the Finn, waited as close to the water as they dared until in half an hour or an hour the boat should return. There was silence on the shore. Once the Sheriff beat the cob bowl in his palm, once the Finn started to point with his cane, stopped. Behind them, silhouetted on the hill, lay the black truck and smoking wagon. The moon was gone.

Bohn listened. His head unerringly followed something across the peaceful water.

"Did you hear that?" whispered the Finn.

"I heard," said Bohn. His eyes were white, he continued to stand despite the pain in his legs. "Keep quiet," he told the Sheriff. And then more softly to the Finn: "You figure they're heading the same way as me?"

He listened for sounds of the three men crouched in the boat, his lips moved as he repeated and memorized a poor stroke of the oars, a word or two that could be recalled and fanned when they returned. "Another fifteen minutes," without looking at the Finn, "and I'm going after them."

"There," whispered the Finn, "is he crazy?"

"I heard," Bohn said again. He watched as if he could see the suddenly phosphorous wake of the rowboat shrinking about its passengers. "I'll burn it," he said.

"Listen," the Finn began to dance on rickety legs, muttered, about to throw himself in the water, "listen!"

The squeak of oarlocks drifted out of the darkness. With every moment Bohn felt the uncertainty of things afloat. The pain in his back, his sore knees, the rubbing wings in his breath flashed sudden signals as he stood still. On the side of his neck a blood vessel began to tick, he abruptly extended his elbow for the Finn to steady. Gradually—and there was no sound, not a tremor except from beyond in the boat—he discovered something which, at his age and no longer able to wait, he could not bear.

"They start up," prodding the Finn, "then stop."

The rowboat turned. "I'll put my foot through it!" Again out of reach they idled and Bohn heard the oars drawn up.

"Over there," whispered the Finn.

Bohn towered on the shore. His legs shook first. Still trying to listen above the sounds of his own body, his hands shook, his arms, shoulders and head wagged as the boat pulled away. He rose in the darkness with rage enough to carry it home on his back.

"What's the matter," the Finn hung to him, "what are they up to, Bohn?"

His mouth opened, a small and lipless zero. With a few short gasps he inhaled and then: "Watch out, Lampson," he cried, "watch out for him!"

The capsized shell of an insect moved bluntly to the pull of oars, resisted the water like an oil drum pushed by pole. From time to time Camper scraped quickly with the can. Crouched on his knees he splashed and twisted his head sternward to catch the speckled fish when it jumped. He jerked fitfully the green thread which lay untouched on the surface.

"I have to reel in again," he said, dropping the can. Furiously he wound the spool.

The little boat clove to the rock side of the dam, for long minutes becalmed in the darkness surrounding the base of the earth, sinking, while the three men sat in it, balanced on the palm of a sodden log. Luke shook himself, lay in the oars. He felt with his eyes into the darkness, searched the rocks, and the ratcheting of the reel stopped.

"There. Don't call to her, she'll scare." Luke pointed. They watched until high above them the close wrapped figure with olive branch took two heavy strides, called, "Mulge," and disappeared. The patched dinghy again trolled its circular way on the vulture's birdbath.

"That's not a rock!" cried Camper when they hit the housetop, and clutched the swaying rod to his chest. "My line'll tangle."

"Perched up here awhile won't hurt you none."

They lay on the flat of the roof. "There's one to the right," Luke swallowed the match flame, the sides of the skull glowed as he cupped his hands. "One out there in the gulch, and another beyond that."

He did not look toward the sunken barns. The hummers, the anxious insects, returned jumping across the water to the house. A broken feather curled along the brim at the back of his head. The small haunches had grown tough, dug into a sandy hillside while his pony slept below.

Cap Leech swept the endless gloss of water, then quickly again to the little man in thong and dust, twisted with a human crick between the fanning oars. He could see nothing of the cowboy's face, only the large oval of the hat like a Quaker's crown.

"He died," said Luke, "and she died and I ain't too keen to remember."

Cap Leech had lost the thermometer. He felt in his pockets, nothing, not a gelatin pill; and he was cold, seated in the bow of a leaky rowboat. Below him lay the empty house with windows uselessly slammed shut at the first warning of the cannon. From one tight sash there floated a wisp of curtain. Inside, a mattress hung in suspension a few inches from the second floor. Behind the house the orchard's tree—transplanted it had never bloomed—remained preserved in the backyard of the lake and waved dimly in its branches the staves and wire of a corselet, the stock of a buffalo gun, a lidless cradle; all tied into the tree for safety, inconceivable that the water could climb that high.

"I been alone since then," said Luke.

Cap Leech stared at the unfamiliar back of the young man drawn up comfortably atop the drowned farm. And he, who by the spoonful or on his handkerchief had shared the opiate slipped to his patients, felt a sudden unpleasant clearness of the head, faced with the foundling plainsman. The first man had died in Eden, they pronounced him dead. And now, with brightening eye, he found himself sitting in the middle of the washed-out garden's open hearth.

140

"Boy." Suddenly he leaned close.

He stared at the tufted head that never turned, at the nape of a soft formed skull the seams of which were not yet grown together, at the lump of ending nerves that was his neck. Man, boy, shard, Cap Leech thought of his eye dilating by its own design, a mean spring opening with surprise, thought of the red rash that would creep along his arms at night from now forward. Within the brainless cord of spinal fluid there was a murky solid, a floating clot of cheerless recognition.

Cap Leech took off his spectacles, wiped, then bent them. He cocked his head, favoring the swelled side of his temple, and in the darkness began to grin through sixty years of accumulated teeth, cut to the gums. Slowly and with the faintest whispering, Cap Leech laughed, his tongue by slight movements pushed and licked each sound, a grim airless ripple so soft as to be hardly heard.

"Watch out, Lampson," hallooing across the water, "watch out for him!"

The boat bubbled at the sides, tipped and sank twenty feet from shore in front of the bystanders, with keel curled and disintegrated, left the men to step out of it under water. They waded to the landing. In single file all stooped and climbed to the top of the hill through the gray ash, the lagging Cap Leech walking with hands clasped behind his back.

"If you had kept quiet," said Camper shortly, "I would have caught one."

Luke said: "We got a wagon already. A trough, a rick, and that ranch house there." He nodded at the upright shadows slanting on One Hundred Acres Grassland and at the Mandan sitting with outstretched legs on the potato bag steps. "The team," listening for a winded snort, "runs free at night." And to the Indian: "Have you seen anybody, Maverick? Been any prowlers on my land?" The door hung open against the wooden, vermiculated wall.

Cap Leech heard the answering harsh sounds of a raven. He climbed down from his little red wagon, stood watching her. Those were abscesses beneath her cheeks, cysts in the Indian pap, which he saw above the hunching of her shoulders and the loose legs brown on top and on the undersides a frog-like white.

"She's been here since a child," said Luke.

Cap Leech walked once around his wagon, brushing the roman nose, and again looked at the Mandan through spectacles hammered tightly under his eyes. He turned, rattled the padlock, and slipped inside, a small old man accused of carrying about the countryside a circus of skin suckers. He was a medical tinker and no longer wore his half face in the fishbowl light of an amphitheater. He put his hands to the hot stove. If there was one last operation to perform, he thought, what would it be, since he had spread anatomy across a table like a net and crumpled with disgust a pair of deflated lungs into a ball. There was none he knew. If a single body could bear all marks of his blade and if it carried only the organs of his dissection, his life work would seesaw across the floor under tresses of arms and ventricles hung from the shoulders, would turn the other emasculated cheek. Slowly he rolled his sleeves and reaching around the stove dropped celluloid cuffs on the bunk tumbled with newspapers and a khaki blanket.

"Come up here," peering from the wagon as through the lifted slats of a pawnshop, and the Indian's dusty hand crept to her shoe. "Here," he repeated, pointing at a spot on the soapy planks between his feet. His eyes blinked as if in a moment's pause he had been defied by a dog which, turned on its back in the shade, shook loose paws over a row of ugly dugs exposed like buttons. Cap Leech merely twisted about and began, knees rustling, to prepare.

He himself had never been hospitalized except in his own wagon and under his own wandering eye. No one had ever, behind a film-like screen, looked at the hairlined features of a body fixed without back or front after the last rheumatic seizure, nor watched, prying at the insides of a virgin relic, the passage of a bismuth cud down ducts that were peculiarly looped and unlike the intestines of either bird or man. It was his pleasure never to bathe at the side of the road.

He had reduced all medicine to a ringed wash basin and kept, for its good or harm, the tinkling world in a bundle under his rocking bed. In the stove he burned powders to kill disease; he lived in useless fumigation. He bled strangers in a room they could not stand in or laid them on his own iodoform dampened quilt. Treatment was his secret and while breathing into a bearded face he remembered the startling slant of a physician's eye through a hole in a steel reflector.

Once he had nearly died in the wagon, naked on a pile of clothing and an arm's length from a bogus bottle of capsules lying on its side without cork or label. To die like a gypsy with a bit of pumice and mercury in a wicker basket—and the horse would have continued on the walk of its choice, craned its head for low apple branches across the road, dragged his body along the borders of unoccupied, lazy states. Not now, the horse stood still and Leech, despite one empty cavity in his abdomen, wiped his hands and with more vigor than ever mixed his scant tools with a hoot in the night.

Out came the tin can. The big eyes of the Indian lay on the sill, she sniffed the heady gas. "This is a xyster," said Cap Leech climbing again to his feet. He had kindled wood with it. For a moment he turned it over, then facing her quickly, "xyster," he repeated and dropped it, the clank of a museum piece, into the enamel pan. "No bone drill," speaking clearly and with a faraway cut to his spectacles, "that's gone."

Back and forth went the can, its lid clapping with the niggardly puffs of a censer. Simultaneously, the Madan's two hands rose a few inches from the arms of the chair, fat dark fingers spread into perfect, electrified starfish. And Cap Leech, with the sparsest gold in his teeth, slid along the wall, fixed the white sheet over the already bolted door.

There was a beginning, a middle, and finally a scrubbing down of the wagon. The mere steam of a croup kettle set him in mind to pay a visit and was enough to recall one by one his pictures of the great troop of the afflicted. He was a midnight vivisectionist in a cat hospital. When the kettle sang there was no stopping until the point was put to flesh. The little ribs clicked along the backs of his hands, he looked at them and then at the Indian who would sit for him until he ended on his knees with a pail and lick of sponge.

"That's bad. That feculence buries itself in the root and then one night it comes out in the brain. Even the black salve won't stop it."

The beginning was nothing but a look into his pockets, a tug on the vest, a pacing now and then interrupted with a quick, open mouthed inspection. It was a moment of osmotic consideration when, from the vantage of his long walk across broken backs, he could again with serious brows glance down upon the undecided paths of youth. Even when he was only thinking of what he would do to her, before the old deftness came into his warty fingers, he was a man apart, not to be disturbed. So cheerfully preoccupied that when the wagon shook he merely steadied himself with a violinist's precious hand. And when they shouted, "Come on out of there. We're going to steal your horse," he simply put his ear to the wood and nodded.

From the darkness Bohn challenged the wagon, his mastiff voice close upon the back steps. "Ho, Doc, we're going to kill the Finn."

But Leech was already to the middle of the one last operation. Slippers padding, pushing the pan near with his toe, he gripped the Indian's face to his hip. Smashes of greasy hair rubbed the smoking vest. "Black salve . . . won't help."

Bad breath, his whole failing system came through his open teeth, second only to the ether. It was the odor of a lopsided, glistening face, the smell of air tasted in advance before it leaves the blood-stream. Closer, that taint of breath, always absorbing, draining, smelling of a dozen others, it clicked short then commenced again with spores and a squinting whistle. He breathed off the aroma of a poultice. The crook stayed in his arm until he was done.

Not once did the Indian with violet pudendum close her eyes. A shifting of the fat woman leg tops, a twitch of the jingling body and she was still, reaching upward mutely a dark spot on her forehead. The ether, tilted under her nose as if he would make her drink, slowed the rise and fall of the sweatered chest, brought no unconsciousness.

Leech staggered coldly with it himself, pulled her into a better light. The pitch of his bland probing, the ether jag height of diagnosis was upon him and he began, pressing the lip, to make out the selected crooked shell as with a red line.

Once more there was the squawk of wheels, a thudding against the wagon and Cap Leech's hold was jarred. Sensing the cut of leather, the tramp of feet, he felt the shafts fall dead and knew that the wagon was no longer powered.

"Finn, can you climb up there alone?"

Only the far voice of falling animals, the inconsequential distraction of merry fleas. His mouth worked, he let the backs of his trousers fan to the stove a moment, bent down once more and with blank face looked into the Indian's pulsing gullet. A few quick movements and he had passed over the crushed strawberries on her breasts.

The elbow remained contracted, unbreakable and hard, tensed as with some nerve disorder, hooked in the invisible sling. He felt no tiredness in that passive arm hypnotically closed on the Indian's head. It waited while the lively fingers of the other hand fished as into the mouth of a bottle and massaged. Once, twice, he pushed at the tooth, curiously, a squatted child pushing his finger into the ribs of a drowsing dog. With mathematical patience he tried its give: nothing,

147

deep through the jaw. Then he stopped, cocked his ear toward her, suspicious, listening.

Emanations. With hovering hand this time interrupted, Leech became aware of the trick. The Indian, in a last bodily defense, slightly bulged some muscles, loosed others, and secreted from licentious scent spots and awakened nodes, a sensation of difference marvelous as anything he had ever seen. The captive, still watching him with unchanged eyes, generated like an octopus the ink of desire. He could see not even a garter, there were no words, not a gesture, but he knew his momentary pause was measured against some beating in her inward temples. A thorough discoloration, a pointed glowing of hidden skin for the old man, and it led him a few steps away, among the moistened ferns. She was waiting to see if he would strike.

"Ride for a fall, Finn," outside there came a four footed whispering from the bronc stockade, "they's burrs in that saddle!"

Cap Leech heard it. But he began.

He carried a face with the jaws clamped at his breast and against the weak spot, a freakish indentation, of his missing rib. The tooth crumbled. No bigger than the eye of a bird frozen to a twig, it splintered, broke apart, as he gauged with the tip of the instrument, worked with a strong twisting of the wrist. Leech applied a woodcarver's rhythm to the crown and neck of the belated thirty-second tine. Now and then the metal, in its circular and steady thrust, touched her lip or knocked against her other teeth.

Often, out of earshot of lonely houses, he had picked miniature incisors from children with only the slightest bleeding, often he had lifted some powerless smooth stone from a senseless gum, but this was a tooth long since died crookedly, the snag shaped microscopic carrot nearly upside down. Behind him ash lumps rustled in the fire, amorphous gray flames walked with suction cups around the stove's inward belly. From beyond the wagon came a sudden soprano quailing, a meaningless "yip, yip, yip," the singing scream. But now, faced with the incomplete incision, having taken the liberty of nursing a flower of tubes from pubescent flesh, he longed only for extraction and the cautious, painful closing of her mouth.

He pulled and the lower half of the Mandan's face followed the swing of his arm, then back again, elastic, cross-eyed, an abnormal craning of the skull to the will of its tormentor, stretched sightless over the shoulder with each plaguing timeless yawl. Leech pulled in waltz-like slow arcs, now breaking the pressures of motion to apply a series of lesser, sharp tugs which caused the Indian's head to nod obstinately up and down and one knee, wide and soft, to fold slowly backward into the privy bronze stomach.

He pried between the overlapping rows with a firebrand. Small, impersonal fingers dipped in foraminous jelly. The ether can spilled into the girl's lap, rolled on the wood. And Cap Leech, after the pincers slipped and marked a blood blister on the inside of her cheek, danced a few gnome-like steps, shuffled quickly, and held the stubborn bedeviled fragment up to the light.

"Outside."

He looked for a moment at the eyes which still unflickering pointed toward the low door. He looked at the raised skirt and, hardly believing, at the mouth from which he had just withdrawn and through which in a single word the girl had spoken. The little vertical creases came again into his face. He stooped, moved, and obeyed, helping her up and to the door, down the steps and into the darkness where she disappeared to some earthen nest or hole where she would recover, packing the wound with clay, or not.

Cap Leech drifted to the front of the wagon where the red tipped springy shafts lay bent to the left, wheels stopped dead in an unfinished sudden turn, kicked the wood lightly and hunched off toward the out buildings. He stood still a moment in the black yard and, feet apart, hands in pockets, peered into the dizzy triangulated night. Between heaven and earth not a rattling cough as he moved and approached the barn.

Wood, sapless, creosoted, he smelled it briefly anchored to the leveled sand. Whatever grass there was grew like a fire at the edge of a ditch along the uneven beginning of the barn floor, a few blades trickling inward between cracks in the faintly urinated planks; a clump also at the bottom of one adjoining fence post. He looked up at, listened to, the open loft. A bundle of unused hay sat there across the brittle arms of a stored and dusty rocker.

Leech stepped toward the barn, away from it, knowing scarcely where to begin, but feeling all the while—there were cicadas under his feet, over to the rise a redolent horse face in the sand—as if he were treading a place of windgall. Back again, softly, he peered inside, craned. There were the bins and roosts, pigeon holes for the ghosts of an animal world under an unsafe roof, all the bitter windings of a fence to be restrung or left barbed in the corner; here he could listen to the twilight of newborn field mice or hide wrapped in a litter of old ropes.

He heard the strut of a rooster. And Cap Leech, hardly beneath the scratching rafter, turned to the moonlit yard.

It mounted to the light with unkempt saddle hack and broken spurs, with an aged flitting leapt between rails and sidled to a remembered mark in the clay. Black sickle feathers hung on the air. The rooster poked, flinched with one talon as if exactly picking over the spot for a certain needle or feeling for a white grain. The aggressive, powdery bird began to twist its neck, cocking the eyes into a startled question, and the wattles fell to the side of the head. Again and again it inflicted upon itself some senseless doubt as the unjointed finger swept over the ruts and maggots.

Then it threw back the stunted limb atop the skull and paced the diameter of the pond, stepping now and then into the blackness and reappearing on the opposite side to hark again toward the center. It dropped one long feather in its tracks from the thinning tail bunch. It could not stay for long in the ring nor too long in shadow, marched before the barn dusting the downy leggings.

The rooster suddenly began to run, a companionless skipping around the circle, and passed the barn each time with averted head and one lifted, rejecting wing. The spared fowl with the comb who could not crow sped with a lunacy to cover its path, and when it slowed at several quarters of the circle it appeared that it would stop on the other side of the yard and beyond reach of the red fox. But the end of the circle brought it to a standstill before the barn, motionless for breath. Then the scabious old cock walked deliberately to the wagon entrance.

Cap Leech was unable to spread his arms or retreat into the passage of webbed stalls. He waited before this dwarfed image, until as it drew close, indifferent now to watching beasts or stones in its way, it finally bumped his ankles and hurtled itself, the midget incubus, to the far stanchion with an imaginary thump.

The beak, the breast, the screw wound shanks and brass toes grew cold against his legs before the black ball flew from under his feet and he escaped the barn.

Leech could hang that bird from a hook. With one stroke, a cupping of the wand hand, he could withdraw the rooster's coiled meld while it died vertically on the wall. He was the dismantler of everything that flew or walked or burrowed at the base of a tree—he could not stand peacefully in the barnyard accepting his eviction by the chicken. So he crept again toward the beam where it had fallen. A slow, noncommittal clucking and the barn held over him its dusty peak, a shadow closing upon the doors rolled aside for the passing of some nocturnal elephant or roach. He felt, in the rags of the chicken thief scratching the grated wire of darkness through which the prowler glides, that he was guided by the slippery fingers of one who carries a gunny sack, a hood, for the squatting quarry.

The bird was hiding. He could hear the wind chortle in its gullet, then the sudden tripping of hooked feet, the flurry of straw against the wing bow as it moved, re-took its position. He waved out-lifted hands, barring its flight as if the cock could stay in the air long enough to escape, and pushed to the rear where one jump would land him on the sudden squawk.

There was no hen house, no setter walking on her breast over abundant eggs, nor was the one-legged guardian posted windward on the gable. Cap Leech did not have to climb, only explore each changing, still warm niche, approach with velvet crouching feet. In and out of a child's late cradle, perched for a moment on the rim of an enamel pitcher, then behind it, pink helmet in full view; it adorned a tilted dry commode and backed off bowing and scraping.

He thought of the face, all nib, and followed the body, the simplest shape, a bag for the intestines, as it puffed and shrank. He stopped, clapped his hands twice and listened as it fell over and over itself. He climbed through the collars, the leather loop, harness for a whale, until he saw the plumes and heard the ligatures and chalk of the bare head batting against the wall. Down came his two stiff arms as one.

Out of the barn slid a short dark tousled figure who carried a handful of tight feathers around the side to the fence and who, moving to his moonlit chores, tossed it over the rails for the horses. Then, crossing the yard briskly, he disappeared into the cabin.

He undressed in front of the open door and by the smudged light of the hurricane lamp. Off came the vest with a careful crick of the arms, picking the buttons, dropping another bit of white cloth to the floor, and there was no curiosity for the place upon whose husks and hides they had slept so long switching their faces. With an old maid agility he skipped into the nightshirt. He left the light smoking for his sons. He tested the bed. And, with low white neckline and tremulous drawstrings, thin loose cuffs and deckled folds, fluttering like a small moth, Cap kicked off his slippers, lay flat, drew the blanket to his chin. Arms straight at his side he slept, waiting, eyes boring through the roof.

My place.

"Shall we let him go," shouting above the engine, "or take him to the hollow?"

"Put me down!" And Camper watched the crusty truck jog from sight. Alone, dun flies dropping from his collar, he began to run toward the dormitory where his wife—wet trouser legs ran faster— had met the fiends.

"I told you to keep that shade drawn. I told you." Even now they might be circling for another look, the amphibiotic eyes. She sat by the child's cot side, feet tightly together, hands folded in her lap. She shook her head. The boy lay on his sheet of white canvas, without fever or chill, the short body draped from top to foot in the translucent gauze of a mosquito net. It clove to the pointed face and thinly hid the open lips. The snake's breath hung about the body.

Camper went to the other cot, stood over it, reached beneath the pillow for the revolver. "Pearl handle," he thought turning it over, still seeing the child's face cut from stone outlined under the white stocking mask, "it ought to have a pearl handle." Fumbling, for useless protection, he stuffed the pistol butt-down in his pocket.

And at last the woman got up, crossed the room, and pressed herself against the open window. For Lou the road to the hills was cut with barbed barricades and red lanterns, or through hundreds of miles of shrub and sand, was stopgapped at little towns. There, become the possession of local officers, it slowed cars to a standstill and subjected travelers to the arm of a wry sheriff. And the gritting voice, sharp jowls and eyes picked over the bodies of those who fled. The driver was taken from his car, the deputy posted with his wife.

"Why, you ain't from around here! You've brought that woman just a piece too far, mister."

The deputy kept a yellow stained hand on the door. "Lady, if he ain't really your husband, it's too late now. And if you ain't always been as pretty as you say, God help you."

Stocks greasy from unshaved cheeks, rubber padded rifle butts and hair triggers met any couple fool enough to show their faces in that hell's place twice. "Mister, if you ever made any money off her, you better give it here."

The deputy was the tallest and craned to the window: "Well, then, what about you, lady?"

When again she looked it was as if her face was on the other side of the screen, solemnly her nails scratched a waiting tattoo on the wire mesh. She whispered and for a moment he could not move. A soft, unfamiliar, lucid condemnation: "Take me out of here."

The gasoline burner sidled down the shale. Brake bands smoked, springs lightly bent, probing. Only the sound of changing gears and an airy pumping of the engine, the flapping of a pulmotor, followed it through the darkness. The mechanical mule felt hoof by hoof for the running scent, balking downward through the young everglade.

"Where are they?"

"Fu'ther."

Bohn himself sat at the wheel. "If I don't get a shot, Sheriff," stamping the pedals with big boots, "I'll be coming in to Clare." The truck dropped around cover of a boulder, descended into the bog. Three men peered through the isinglass with itching fingers.

"Kill most anything tonight." And after a silence he muttered, "Bound to. In Saggitarius."

"Keep going, Bohn," said Luke.

In the back of the hunting truck, lolling against the cab, Wade cradled the weapons across his lap, and into each, gazing up at the black heat or turning to look through splintered slats, attracted by some flipping tail under the wheels, he carelessly inserted two twelve gauge bulging shells, the lumps of explosive wadding. "I ain't going to blow my head off," he thought and waved away with fat hands the longest barrels. The shells had golden, corroded crowns, rusty paper shanks. "Is this one here fixed, or isn't it?" His long hide shoelaces danced on the wood, he clapped a hand on the ammunition box.

The driver, now full of the smells of duck congealed canvas, allowed himself a mouthful of the tar-layered plug for the better taste of game. Gasoline, tobacco, death, he felt the satisfied warning in his groin.

And Luke: "Bohn, bite me off a piece."

Down they came with switching sensitive ears and a mania for scouring the crabbed hiding lands below the dam, rucksacks ready for the first bag. The loose disconnected eyes of the truck turned one way then the other, goaded over the fresh foot holes.

"I didn't bring no carbines. Buckshot'll do."

Haunch up, falling haunch, they nuzzled the beating bush, silent again as the suckless engine geegawed cautiously into the hollow: that intense silence of set jaw and frown, waiting to pick up the scratching of a bird's ear. Strain, and they perspired, three abreast on the front seat, lips tasting the far-off fur. Sand splattered over the lead wrapped wire through a hole in the floor boards. Wade carried peaceably his load of metal cordwood. He did not like noise.

The gray truck chugged to a stop before Eve's slimy pool, an un-shielded dip of water in the waves of earth that, as far as they could see, appeared to be covered with palm leaves, broad, clay-veined shadows. Bohn climbed down, filled the canteen, tasted the water. The back of his head filled the window, one foot cocked on the mended running board. "Oil," speaking over his shoulder, spitting, "they come this way all right."

"We'll set here and wait for them," said Luke.

But once again they prowled forward, scattered abandoned nests and crossed small bodies of quicksand. Bohn pushed the truck further into the squeaking rushes.

Rum breath, saddle pants, and rank signs through the forest of needles; they did their hunting at night, dragged through roadless quagmires, and trundled under the dusky bluffs of Mistletoe. The black face hunters hooked rosined fingers in their belts, stared about bitterly for the undiscovered lairs. Suddenly, through the briars, they heard the coughing of another engine.

"There," Bohn pulled the brake, "that's them!"

"Switch on the lights." And through the whorls of milky under-growth they saw the troop of Red Devils on little horned motorcycles.

"You shoot," cried Wade, "I ain't going to shoot!"

"Load them guns."

They fell from the cab and with ragged trouser bottoms, sealed grins, clamored over the sidings and dropped by Wade. Shells spilled under their feet.

"Hit them now," Bohn pillowed the butt into his shoulder, drew down his head, "or never."

They fired. From the parapet of the truck a tinkling cloud of shot landed among the vandal herd, rock salt into the buttocks of cornered apple thieves. In the headlights and streaming of the muskets, one motorcycle, as its rider fled, turned to flame under the little seat, reared, contorted into a snake embrace, and fell writhing in fire. A honking set up from the handless horn as the rubber bulb shrank in the heat.

Flat shells, smoke, recoil filled the truck, one side ablaze with the spitting triple battery. Bohn's cheek was blue and red, a great wattle under the punishment of the gun, his eye steely down the barrel. In his corner, taking aim, Luke trained upon the dancing throng and with pinched mouth, bile rising from his stomach, held his fire.

"Shoot," a voice at his ear, and he pulled the trigger.

The Devils limped under the red ball rain, suddenly pirouetted into the air or, taking one cleft step, dropped punctured and deflated, arms curling then flat on the ground. One jumped to his machine and Luke, again readying for the painful blow, looked full into the enormous reflecting goggles, the startled stare, and watched the dovetailed shot fan wide. Calmly he wiped the floating smoke from the muzzle.

Some mounted and in graceful frenzy drove head on toward the truck, beat their skinny jointless arms. Luke watched them coming, the Devils skimmed across his sights, kicked up their wheels. With blue powdered hands he gripped the carved wood stock, the hammered, tarnished silver, and he drank the waves of Bohn's sweaty firing. He saw nothing but the nugget on the end of the gun, cross-eyed

157

at the bead, watching it circle of its own will and apart from any target. . .

"Lead them. They fly too fast for dead on aim. Swing your arms."

His eye crept along the hexagonal gun metal. There was no cotton in his ears, nothing to dull the slapping of air on either side as Bohn and the Sheriff discharged their weapons into the belly of the dam. The sweep before the truck was filled with leaves perforated and lightly touched by the swarms of buckshot. He crooked a finger on the sticky trigger. He reached out for ammunition. Then: "This is for one. And this is for another."

He could feel the eruption under his nose before he squeezed; he fell back with the mistake, the searing, double dinosaurian footfall of the twin bores.

And suddenly, from the isolated battering truck, shrill and buoyant above the clumsiness of thick-kneed marksmen, there came that cool baying of the rising head, the call to kill, louder and singsong, faintly human after the flight of Devils, the nasal elated sounds of the cowboy's western bark.

Yip, yip, yip.

CAP LEECH

now *I'll talk.*

You've answered to me for having found him crouched with bare, folded feet, for having watched the thinly wrinkled, perforated breath of skin that was his throat—dry now, untouched, except for the soothing pressure of some tons of earth—for having spied on the wrappings, the colorless cloth, the complete expulsion of bodily fluids, the immobility of ten dangling fingers shoved like minnows into the shriveled ground.

One town further then: last seen by a river peering upward into his lumpy jaws.

Take me there.